SURFERS OF SNOW

W9-BEQ-520

Copyright © 1998 Kim Askew

ALL RIGHTS RESERVED. No part of this book may be reproduced in any
manner without the express written consent of the publisher, except in the
case of brief excerpts in critical reviews and articles. All inquiries should be
addressed to Fitzhenry & Whiteside Limited, 195 Allstate Parkway,
Markham, Ontario, L3R 4T8. (e-mail: godwit@fitzhenry.ca)

First published in the United States in 1999.

Fitzhenry & Whiteside acknowledges with thanks the support of the
Government of Canada through its Book Publishing Industry Development
Program in the publication of this title.

Printed in Canada.
Design by Kerry Designs
Cover Illustration: John Mardon

10 9 8 7 6 5 4 3 2 1

Canadian Cataloguing in Publication Data

Askew, Kim
Surfers of Snow

ISBN 1-55041-379-1

I. Title

PS8551.S556S97 1998   C813'.54   C98-931320-4
PR9199.3.A84S97 1998

SURFERS OF SNOW

KIM ASKEW

Fitzhenry & Whiteside

For Mum and Dad

With special thanks to
Deirdre Currie, Michele Phillips, Christine Triggs, and Tom Valis

CHAPTER 1

Pain shot up my thigh as I hoisted my lower body off the ground and into the waiting rescue toboggan. Brent, the older of the two Ski Patrollers, gently maneuvered my right leg into position, taking care not to disturb the already swollen knee. Despite his care it was throbbing like mad.

"Guess this takes you out of action for a while, eh, Tanner?" he said to me in his Irish accent, as he wrapped a gray army blanket around my legs in preparation for transporting me down the hill.

"Looks that way. How's my board?" I asked. I was cursing inside. In the dim, flat light I hadn't seen that ridge of rock showing faintly gray beneath a layer of fresh snow. Now my knee was wrecked and my board was probably trashed.

The other patroller, one I hadn't seen around before, picked up my snowboard and turned it over. "It's got a pretty good gouge in it," he said, flipping it around for me to see. "You're lucky you weren't hurt worse than you are, you know. You and those snowboarding friends of yours are getting out of control, taking too many risks. You guys better clean up your act before one of you gets yourself killed. We've been having enough problems on this mountain lately without having to worry about a bunch of reckless kids on snowboards."

"Yeah, whatever," I said, lying back and closing my eyes. Guys like him had no clue what snowboarding was all about. Most riders I know become hooked on snowboarding right from the start, like it is some kind of drug. It grabs you somehow, and riding a board down a mountainside becomes a total source of, I don't know, energy or pride or inspiration or something. It was the kind of thing you immediately understand – or you never did. Simple as that. I've learned that it was a waste of time trying to explain the magic of it to those who just didn't get it.

"Can you take me down now?" I asked. "I'd better call somebody to come and pick me up."

I was surprised to find out that Brent hadn't finished lecturing me either, since his son ran the best snowboard shop in town and he usually stood up for riders.

"Jeff does have a point," he said. "I hear that Area Management is worried about liability. They don't want to get sued and they won't be turning a blind eye to these shenanigans like they have in the past." He looked down at me as he strapped on his skis and shrugged. "It's not our call, Tanner. All right. Let's go."

I felt the toboggan slide sideways a bit as the two patrollers skillfully traversed through the soft new snow back to the packed main trail and headed down to the chalet. I looked up at the gray layer of clouds. Damned light.

My mom didn't freak out at all, which was a relief. She just drove over in our battered four-wheel-drive station wagon to pick me up and take me to the clinic. She used to get upset and threaten to stop me from using my board, but she's developed a tougher attitude towards my various cracked ribs, concussions and bruises. This time she just asked me how badly

2

it hurt and then she and Brent helped me hobble over to the car and get settled across the back seat, which was covered in dog hair. Mom was actually smiling a little as she spoke to Brent before getting in the car and starting the engine.

It's been just me and my mom for about seven years now, since I was nine. We moved from the city to Sighing Pass right after the divorce. She teaches grade five at the elementary school, and I'm in grade eleven at Sighing Pass Secondary School. My dad still lives in the city, two hours away, and I see him sometimes. Life in the city is so different from life in the mountains, though. I don't think he really understands how things have changed for us.

At the clinic, the doctor manipulated my knee back and forth. "Does this hurt?"

"A lot," I acknowledged. "It feels like something's rubbing inside."

"That could be fluid accumulating as the joint swells," said the doctor. "I don't think it's too serious. You may have temporarily dislocated your kneecap, and you've probably pulled some ligaments. Keep off it for a few days while the swelling goes down and ice it as often as you can. Then we should also think about getting you started on some physiotherapy."

"When can I snowboard again?" I asked.
The doctor stopped writing in my file and looked at me. "That depends, Tanner," he said, a bit sternly. "But remember, you can't rush nature, and if you do, you're going to end up with a knee that will take a long, long time to heal."

"Can Tanner get the physiotherapy here?" asked Mom.

"Well," the doctor frowned, "he can work on some exercises, but what he really needs is ultrasound therapy. He'd have to go to the city for that. Would that be possible?"

My mom nodded. "If that's what he has to do."

She was quiet in the car on the way home. She asked me once if I wanted an aspirin for the pain, but I don't like to put chemicals in my body and besides, it didn't hurt all that much anymore.

"You don't want me to go to the city, do you?" I asked her.

She frowned, but didn't take her eyes off the road. "No, it's not that at all," she replied. "If that's where the best physiotherapy is, then that's where you should go. It's the driving I'm worried about. It's nearly two hours each way, and with the winter weather being so unpredictable, I don't know how we'll get you there and back without missing a lot of school."

Missing school didn't sound like such a loss to me but I did have another suggestion. "You don't have to drive me every time, Mom," I told her. "I can stay with Dad and I can telecommute to school. I'll set it up with my homeroom teacher and I won't miss anything. We'll work it out."

Mom took a hand off the wheel to rub her eyes and looked at me, smiling. "I know, I know," she said. "We always do."

4

CHAPTER 2

Mom and I have been working stuff out since she and my dad split. Mom never liked the city much and after the divorce we kind of gravitated here. She's pretty cool, as mothers go. She's young and pretty in a natural kind of way. She never wears makeup and she's really fit. She used to ski race when she was a girl and she taught me to ski almost before I could walk. When snowboarding came along, she wouldn't let me get one because she thought it was just a fad, and when I started coming home all beat up from wiping out on a borrowed board she nearly put her foot down. She let me keep doing it, though. She said she admired how hard I struggled to improve and now she thinks it's great that I snowboard. There's a bit of a rebel in her, at least that's what my dad says. He can't figure out why she'd leave the city to live in a little chalet on the mountain with only me and the dogs for company.

I could hear the barking as the car turned into the drive. Although our neighbor had ploughed it out for us, the snow had drifted in and blurred the edges. It was slow work limping up the walkway to the chalet, and when Mom opened the door the dogs nearly knocked me down.

"Down, Sherpa! Down Connor!" Mom commanded them. Sherpa is my mom's favorite, a bizarre cross between an

Australian Shepherd and a Husky. She has blue eyes and a crazy patchwork coat of brown, white and bluish swirled fur. Connor is my dog, a big Golden Retriever with a thick, reddish gold coat and deep brown eyes. They were so excited to see us their tails were thumping into everything: the walls, my crutches, my sore knee....

"Ooww!" I yelped.

"That's it," Mom said. "You two are going outside." She herded them out into the snow. "They've got so much affection to give, they might do you more harm than good."

I looked around at our chalet, the wood stove with the fire nearly out, the hardwood floors all scuffed from the dogs' paws, the two big sofas. All of a sudden I felt very, very tired.

Of course, I was a spectacle on my crutches the next day at school. Our school is small, with only one class per grade. Crowds of people visit Sighing Pass on weekends and holidays, but the size of the year-round community is more like that of a small town. You can ski six months of the year here. My teacher, Mr. Ryerson, says that tourists are the lifeblood of this town, but most of the locals pretend to barely tolerate the outsiders. My friends and I called the city people *haoles*, which is a Hawaiian word for outsider. After all, we're the locals and Sighing Pass is really our turf.

I met up with the other surfers before class started. There were four of us: Jonas, Trevor, Xavier, and me. We called ourselves the Surfers of Snow, or SOS, (which also stands for "Save Our Souls" in old-fashioned Morse code), because all of us felt snowboarding was the most amazing thing we'd ever tried and we couldn't imagine life without it. We knew the best runs on the mountain, the best places to build a kicker, and we were getting pretty hot in the halfpipe. We were all locals, although the longest any one of us had lived here was seven years. Except for Xavier, we started snowboarding at about the same time, and we hung out together, hacking around on skateboards and mountain bikes in the summer and barely coming indoors all winter.

Xavier, or Xav for short, was new to our mountain, but he was the best rider I knew, especially on the really steep stuff. Xav came from France. We thought he was a total geek at first. He dressed differently than we did and he always wore glasses with thick black frames. He was skinny, and I mean so skinny you could see his ribs. Of course, he started getting picked on at school right away. I don't remember any of the Surfers joining in, but I'm pretty sure we didn't exactly try to stop it. I do remember that we teased him a little by copying his French accent. Then one day we spotted him coming down a couloir, take a five-meter jump off a cornice and land it perfectly - and that's when we started thinking differently. Xav's been skiing and boarding all kinds of crazy stuff in the Alps ever since he was a little kid, and his dad runs a helicopter skiing operation in town called Alpine Air. Originally we thought we'd do Xav a favor and let him hang out with us, but things sort of happened the other way around. We ended up tagging along behind him and asking him to show us how he did all his cool tricks. All of us could speak some French (we have to learn it in school) and Xav's English was pretty good, so we didn't have too much trouble communicating. Now we use a kind of mix of both languages.

"Bummer, Tanner," remarked Trevor in his usual blunt manner, as I hobbled over to where they were standing. Trevor didn't mince his words. He always said exactly what was on his mind but was rarely drawn into an argument or a fight.

It was good to have a guy like him around. He was tall and had sandy brown hair and gray eyes. He'd been working out with weights in his basement since he was thirteen years old and he had the best build of all the Surfers. He also looked the oldest. He could pass for nineteen easily if it weren't for the braces he still wore on his teeth. He played on the school football team and he used to play hockey back before he started snowboarding. Now, like the rest of us in winter, he was devoted to the board.

"C'est dommage," commiserated Xav.

"Bad things come in threes," said Jonas, staring down at his baggy jeans and Airwalks sneakers. "That's two."

"What do you mean?" I asked. "What else happened?"

"I tried to call you last night, but your mom said you were crashed out." Jonas looked up, tossing his long blonde hair out of his eyes. "You didn't hear about Trevor's board; it got carved up."

"What?"

"Someone carved a big X in the base of my board," explained Trevor. "It's totally trashed."

"Who do you think did it?" I asked.

He shrugged. "Skiers, haoles probably. It's no secret they hate us."

"Yeah, but wrecking someone's board seems a little extreme. What are you going to do? Can it be fixed?"

"I took it to Mike's shop to see if he could do something," he replied. "I don't know though. Whoever it was did a pretty good job of trashing it. What a drag. I was really psyched for the contest."

I felt a sudden constriction in my chest. The contest. I'd forgotten about it. It's not an official contest, it's actually kind of a secret. The local snowboarders get together to show off their talent on some of the wildest, most extreme terrain on the mountain. A few of the older guys from town come back from the States or from wherever they've been traveling to do the judging. With snowboarding practically a subversive activity on the mountain these days, contests like ours are the kind of thing that keep the brotherhood alive. And now with my knee messed up...I might not even get to enter.

"Eh! Class is starting! We are late." Xav's voice brought me back to reality. We headed in across the yard.

CHAPTER 3

My teacher, Mr. Ryerson, was pretty understanding about the whole situation. When I went to the city to stay with my dad, I would telecommute to Sighing Pass Secondary School using my dad's computer. Mr. Ryerson agreed to e-mail the assignments to me and I would e-mail my work back to him. We were doing a lot of independent study anyway, so I could continue my research on the Internet at my dad's place as well as I could at school.

It was the last period of the afternoon, geography. I looked around at the other kids in the class. Jonas was chatting with Sue, new to Sighing Pass school and already one of the more popular girls at school. He had such an easy way with the females it made me sick. In a small town everyone knows everyone, and in Sighing Pass, aside from the haoles, who came and went, newcomers got noticed. Jonas would be the first to say "I saw this babe boarding up on the Bear Run, saw her downtown a couple of times too." And then he'd be introducing us to his new girlfriend. I noticed the cute ones too, I just didn't go up to them as casually and start talking to them. But Jonas, with his long blond hair and surfer looks, was a magnet for girls.

I've gone out with a few girls in high school, but never for very long. There was no one that I was really interested in at school at the moment, nor did anyone seem particularly interested in me. I didn't have Jonas' California good looks and I never got giggling girls calling me up, like he did. There was one girl, though, that I kind of met on the Internet. We e-mailed each other all the time, but I hadn't told the guys about her. They think the Net's for nerds. And they could be right. She sounds cool but you never know. That's the scary thing about the Internet. It's so anonymous you could be communicating with someone who seemed totally normal and cool but could actually be a complete weirdo and you'd never know unless you met the person for real.

"Tanner. What is the bearing you need to follow from Point A to Point B?" Mr. Ryerson's voice startled me from my thoughts. I mumbled and focused on the map in front of me. We were looking at topographical maps and how to read them with the help of a compass. I placed the compass on the map lining the edge up with the two points. I turned the compass housing so that the north and south lines on the compass lined up with those on the map. Then I read the bearing the compass indicated.

"132°"

Mr. Ryerson turned to the class. "Tanner can read a compass very well but he's still not going to get to Point B. Why?" Sue's hand shot up. "Yes, Sue?"

"He forgot to account for the declination."

She was right. I had forgotten one very important thing. Reading a compass is actually more complicated than it sounds because compass needles point to magnetic north, not to true north. If you don't live directly south of the magnetic north pole then there's a difference between the two. And in western British Columbia, where we live, there's quite a difference. It's called declination and you need to account for it or you'll get more and more off track the further you go on your compass bearing. The number of degrees you need to add or subtract is printed on most maps. In my head I accounted for the difference between true and magnetic north for the map in front of me.

"118°" I offered.

"That's right." He turned to the class. "It's very easy to forget this but it is extremely important if you are really navigating outside." I put up my hand.

"Yes, Tanner?"

"Why do we need to do all this? Why not use a G.P.S.?"

"Good point. Class, G.P.S. or Global Positioning Satellite Systems don't require you to calculate the declination. They're like electronic compasses that send and receive signals from satellites. All you have to do is program in the coordinates for Point A and Point B and follow the direction the G.P.S. indicates. But there are a few problems for folks like us, Tanner, even if we understand the latest technology."

"Such as?" I asked.

"Do you have $350 for an electronic compass? And what do you do if the battery runs out?" The class laughed. "I guess we still need to learn the old-fashioned way. OK class, for homework, calculate the bearings to each of the other points indicated on the map. It's a skill that might come in useful someday."

I rolled my eyes but started the work anyway, and had most of it done by the time the bell rang.

CHAPTER 4

The Surfers usually head straight for the mountain as soon as school's over, or else we go to Xav's house because he and his Dad have built a kicker in their backyard. Our boards won't fit in our school lockers so to save going home we leave them at Mike's shop, The Edge of Reason, during the day. It's also a cool place to hang out. Mike runs the shop and also works on the Ski Patrol with his dad. The shop carries magazines, gear, clothes and shoes. It's also the best place to hear the latest gossip. Mike put a couple of couches and a Coke machine in the mechanics' area in the back so we can hang out and talk without getting in the way - since it takes us forever to save up enough money to actually buy anything. We almost always have something behind the counter that we're working on paying off. Mike won't let anything leave the store, though, until it's completely paid for. He says that's how we all stay friends.

I pushed open the door with my shoulder and hobbled my way in. It was a complete drag trying to get around on my crutches with all the ice and slush around. The shop was warm inside and there weren't any customers there besides us. I flopped down on one of the couches and laid back.

"Man, I hope I can get rid of these things soon."

"Relax, Tanner," said Mike. "There's lots of winter left."

"Endless winter, eh Mike?" piped in Jonas. He was refer-
ring to some of Mike's legendary trips. Mike had done some
all right stuff before he started the shop. He must have been
nearly thirty, and it wasn't like he tried to act like one of us or
anything, but he had an easy way with us somehow. He
dressed in snowboard clothing, a bit old school though and
mixed with stuff he wore in his surfing days, like Hawaiian
shirts, and he sported a goatee. He used to make these super
long road trips for surfing - following the summer sun right
around the world. He and his friends would spend the summer in California, and then move on to Maui and Oahu for a
few months. If there was enough money, the next stop was
Indonesia and the wilder beaches of Java and Sumatra, followed by the Australian coast. Then, when the money really
ran out, they'd go back home to Mom and Dad's to work for
the spring and make some more money. Then it would start all
over again.

Mike had told us tons of excellent stories. Like how
they'd gotten chased away from the best breaks on the
Hawaiian North Shore and had their tires slashed by territorial
surfers, and about crazy landings on remote beaches in little
airplanes. He'd had a few run-ins with sharks, too. Surfers
don't hang out between the flags of a patrolled beach. They're
further along up the beach where the waves are bigger and the
shore is rocky or lined with sharp coral. From under the water,
a surfer on a board looks a lot like a seal. Mike was actually
nudged by a shark when he was sitting in the line-up one time,
the point just past where the waves start to break. That's
where surfers sit and ride the swell up and down waiting for a
decent set. Then when a good wave comes in they lie down
on their boards, paddle hard, and drop in just as the wave

starts to break. Anyway, this one time there were all these guys sitting out there on their boards and Mike feels someone bang into his board. He turns around to give the guy hell, and that's when he sees the fin. It wasn't any dolphin, either, it was a big tiger shark cruising right along the line-up. Mike said he would never have guessed it was possible for so many surfers to ride the same wave in, but they did, except for a few hard core hippies who thought their karma would protect them. Apparently sharks don't usually attack people all that often. I wouldn't want to test my karma that way.

I tried surfing one summer at Long Beach, on the west coast of Vancouver Island. You could rent surfboards and those shorter ones that you lie on. Vancouver Island isn't California, though. The water is seriously cold and a wet suit is de rigeur. Surfing's not something you can pick up and be good at in just a couple of weekends, like snowboarding. You really need to live near the beach and go out everyday for, like, years, before you're any good at all. I've never swallowed more water in my life. My board kept getting sucked right over the falls and then I'd land on top of it. And even paddling out to the break is hard because you have to force this big fiber-glass board through all the waves breaking on top of you.

Mike used to live down in Santa Barbara where he says the waves were great but the boarding hopeless, so he moved north. He switched over from skiing early and started board-ing on one of the earliest prototypes of the snowboard called the Snurfer. He said the ride was awful, it was impossible to steer and when you wiped out you really trashed yourself.

Mike had been in on the snowboarding scene when it was just beginning. He had known that the Snurfer was the start of something bigger. There were a couple of other snowboard shops in town, but none had the gear and the clothes in stock before they even hit the magazines like Mike's did. He had contacts among his old friends down in California who sent the latest stuff his way.

"Hey, Tanner." I was surprised to see that Mike had my board in his hands. I'd forgotten all about it and must have left it behind the day before. "My dad gave me your board. I heard what happened so I repaired the gouge in the base. It wasn't too bad. The weird thing though, is that the front binding is completely destroyed. It looks like it's been cut through at the base."

I took the board from him and looked at it. "That's bizarre." I ride goofy, with my right foot forward and he was right. My front binding, just a little metal fitting on the board, had been torn off and the raw edge was jagged and shiny. "I just had a tune up."

"That couldn't have happened in a fall," said Mike. "You'd have to use a hacksaw to cut it like that. Look. It's a clean cut to here and then it's been completely ripped off. Where have you been leaving your board?"

I thought back to the day before. I'd ridden all morning, then went in to warm up and eat something, and then went back out and then, yes, it was on my first run when I'd crashed. "I left it outside the chalet..." I shook my head in disbelief. "No way! Why would anyone do that to my board?"

Mike shrugged. "It looks like it's been tampered with. No problem, though. I've got some spare parts here. I can fix it for you. You're better off than Trevor, nothing I could do could repair the damage to the base of his board."

"I tell you, man," said Jonas, "The vibes are bad. Someone's out to get us. I swear."

If only we'd known then how right he was.

CHAPTER 5

In the scene, it's one of those perfect winter days. The sun is shining and the colors of the winter landscape are bright. The only other person with me is Jonas. We are dressed in our snowboarding gear and our boards are strapped to our backpacks. We are hiking up a ridge, but it is not one that I recognize. Jonas is ahead of me and the old-fashioned snowshoes he is wearing leave a criss-cross pattern in the snow. I step in his tracks and loose snow squishes up through the lacing of my own snowshoes.

As we near the top of the ridge, I can look down into the bowl. Snow and ice hang over the edge, forming a huge cornice. There are shadows beneath it that are purple and blue and gray. We are very high up on the mountain. Jonas turns to look at me and the sun glints off the metal edge of the snowboard slung on his back. He's smiling. I can't see his eyes behind his mirrored sunglasses. He points down into the bowl, a hollow expanse of white, cradled on either side by sharply defined black rocks. His lips are moving but the wind blows his voice away. I don't need to hear him, I know what he is saying. "This is the place. We are the only ones here. First tracks will be ours, as if we are spray-painting our names on a freshly painted white wall."

And then I find myself on my board and dropping into the bowl; powder spraying soft as smoke, perfect toe and heel edge turns. I feel no fear. Leaning my body out parallel to the snow, I drag a glove across the surface. I cruise down the mountain. Ahead of me, Jonas rips through the snow, tearing up the slope like a piece of paper. The tearing sound is the first sound I have been able to hear, and it gets louder and louder. Suddenly I feel a rush of fear. I slam on the breaks and scream to Jonas but my voice makes no sound. I can only watch, horrified, as the snow surface from the leading edge of Jonas' last turn breaks away, cutting cleanly across from one side of the bowl to the other. It roars down towards Jonas' rocketing form like a tidal wave. He looks back over his shoulder. His lips are moving but I can't hear what he is saying and in the next instant, he is engulfed.

My body jerked and a sudden pain stabbed my knee. I woke up gasping. I looked around at the walls of my room, the pine furniture, the familiar posters. There was a clicking sound of dog paws on a wood floor and Connor thrust his cold wet nose into my neck. He whined, startled from his own sleep on the rug next to my bed. I wrapped an arm around his neck and hauled him up onto the bed. I'd been having the same dream every night for the last three, and it was starting to freak me out a bit. Connor and I slept until my mom's knock on the door in the morning woke us again.

By Friday I could put some weight on the knee and most of the swelling had gone down. I wished I could swap my stupid crutches for my snowboard; I really missed riding everyday. I guess at first it hurt so much I didn't even want to think about it but once I could shuffle around a bit I felt like a total loser, especially listening to the guys down at Mike's shop.

"You should have seen Xav go off yesterday," said Jonas. "He tore over this five-meter gap and landed it like it wasn't even there."

"It was only three meter." Xav corrected him. Xav wasn't much one for blowing his own horn

"Oh, man. I can't wait for that new board," said Trevor wistfully, eyeing a slick snowboard with a matte black topsheet stashed under Mike's bench.

"It's going to take a lot of pocket money to pay that off," I commented.

"Yeah, as well as two Christmases and a couple of birthdays used up." He smiled. "It took some convincing."

"Any word on when you'll be back out there on the mountain?" asked Mike, busy structuring the base of a board.

"Actually," I answered, "I'm going down to my dad's tonight. I'm gonna stay in the city for a couple of weeks for physio."

"Well, don't rush that knee," he cautioned, looking up from his work. "I know some older guys who really messed themselves up for good, trying to get back out there too early after getting hurt."

"Yeah, I'll be careful."

"Speaking of the older guys, how's the contest shaping up?" He looked around at us.

"I finally got in touch with Bucky and he'll be there," responded Jonas. "He was on a road trip, but I tracked him down in Colorado. Most of the older guys are on the road now, not too many in town these days."

The road trip was considered a right of passage to a lot of snowboarders. After they graduated from secondary school, a lot of them took some time off before they went to university or started working. Often they'd pool together to buy a Volkswagen van or a pick-up truck and then they'd leave for a snowboarding road trip. They'd drive from mountain resort to mountain resort, seeking out the best run, the best snow, the best halfpipe or the cutest girls and stay for a while. You didn't need a lot of money to take a road trip. You'd just crash on someone's floor and they'd do the same when they came to your mountain. It was considered a pretty cool way to spend the winter after graduation.

"The word will get around," I said. "I can ask Betty to post it on that Internet site she found. Only hardcore riders know how to dial in to that."

"Who is this mystery Betty, anyway, Tanner?" asked Jonas, in a mocking tone of voice. "Are you seeing her, or what?"

"Shut up, Jonas," I told him. "It's none of your business."

"OK, man," he said, "but I have my doubts if she's real."

CHAPTER 6

"I don't know how your mother can live here," said my dad, turning his new Lexus onto the highway. "It's so isolated."

"She likes it here," I replied, sinking back into the seat. "She says she feels more connected here."

"Connected to what, I wonder. It's a backwater on both the real and the information highways."

"We've got computers, Dad, in fact we're even on the Internet at school. We've got everything in town we need: stores, restaurants, clinic, movies, arcade, even a dog pound. It's not like we're living in the Stone Age."

"No, more like the Snow Age" he said, looking at me across the front seat. "I'm not sure I like the idea of you hanging around with all those snowboarding friends of yours either. You could be doing something more productive with your time, like getting a part time job or something."

I stared out the car window at the snow-cloaked peaks of the Coastal Range. We were driving along a road with steep rocks soaring up on one side and a sheer drop into the valley below on the other. Sometimes Dad doesn't have a clue. I do odd jobs for cash and sometimes I watch the store for Mike, but that's not really what the conversation was about. Dad's still shaking his head over why Mom left and came here when he thought they had everything. His idea of being disconnected is being without his cell phone. My mom's idea of being disconnected means not having animals around, or watching the seasons change, or having neighbors that you talk to. I was thinking about how different the two of them had become when I heard Dad's sharp intake of breath.

I felt the car swerve sharply and start to skid. I looked up to see an elk bounding across the road in front of us. It was on a collision course with our car!

The car careened across the road. Dad spun the wheel. Suddenly the tires found traction on the icy surface and jerked us sharply into a skid in the opposite direction. Dad wrestled with the wheel, and after fishtailing a few times he slowed the car to a stop. He turned to look at me. His face was white. The elk had disappeared up the steep embankment.

"Are you OK?"

My arms were braced against the dashboard. "Fine," I croaked.

"Damned elk. Come on, let's get out of here."

I didn't look out at the scenery for the rest of the way. Had our car toppled off the road's edge that would have been it for us. Our province has too many kilometers of twisty mountain roads to be able to protect them all with crash-proof barriers. I'd never really thought about it before. The highway had always seemed like a perfectly safe place. It's weird how something so beautiful can be so peaceful one moment and so deadly the next. Had we driven through a moment sooner, the elk would not have yet appeared. A moment later, and we might have hit the cow-sized animal head on, or skidded off the road and plunged over the cliff to our deaths.

An hour or so later we entered the outskirts of the city. I

always feel kind of culture-shocked when I go to visit my dad. There are just too many cars and signs and buildings and too many people with unfamiliar faces. After a few days though, I don't think about it much. My dad loves it there. He's a stock-broker, and he moved from the house we had when I was lit-tle to this deluxe condo downtown. It's all tall metal and glass, with a view of other tall metal and glass buildings all around. You can just barely see a slice of harbor from the window.

"Now, I'm going to be working everyday, but I'll try to get home from the office as early as I can," he said, unfolding a map onto the gleaming kitchen table. "Look here, I'll show you where the physiotherapist's office is. It isn't far, you can man-age it on your crutches, I think."

"Fine," I answered, leaning over the map to see. I'd have to take a bus and then hobble two blocks, not bad. "Dad, is there anything to eat around here?"

"I think so, check the 'fridge," he said, standing up. "I've got some work to do before tomorrow. You can use the com-puter to do your schoolwork and surf the Net or whatever, O.K?"

"Yeah," I said and hopped down the hall to the room Dad keeps for me. It's got new furniture, but also some stuff of mine that I've had since I was a kid and have totally outgrown. Reminds me of a time warp. I pulled an old paperback off one of the bookshelves: The Great Brain, by John Fitzgerald. It used to be one of my favorites. My mom never let me watch much T. V. so I used to read a lot of books. I don't seem to read as much since I started boarding. I mostly just read snow-boarding magazines and surf the Net. Anyway, this book is about a really smart kid who lived in Utah about fifty years ago. He solves all kinds of mysteries, but not like some cheesy do-good crime fighter. Along the way, he always manages to swindle a lot of money out of people for himself.. It's a good book, and after I read it for the first time I wanted to be a con-man. I tried some swindling of my own on my parents and the kids at school - I never got away with it, though. I think people must be a lot more suspicious nowadays. Or maybe I just wasn't clever enough.

I took the book over to my bed. With all the weird stuff that had been happening, I felt more like the Great Brain than ever before. My board rigged, Trevor's trashed, and a whole lot of strange tension in the air in Sighing Pass - maybe it all added up. It was right then and there that I decided if something mysterious was going on, or something big was going down, then I was going to figure out what.

CHAPTER 7

Hey Betty, long time no talk. I pressed enter and waited. I'd been at my dad's for three days and I was messing around on the Internet at the computer in his study. I hadn't logged on in a while, and I could see that Betty had left a couple of e-mails for me.

A bit of an explanation about Betty, which isn't even her real name. It's actually Jenny. Jenny is a frustrated boarder living in the city. She gets out to the local areas on weekends, but none of her friends snowboard so she ends up riding alone a lot of the time. She got into our Internet chat room to hook up with other snowboarders and called herself Betty because she was the only board-betty at her school. We started e-mailing each other, which is private compared to the chat room where everyone can read your stuff, and we managed to keep in touch over the summer and fall. She's pretty cool: goes to high school in the city, rides all she can, and works at a coffee shop. She finally gave me her real name, but I still haven't actually met her in person.

I checked my watch. It was about the time we usually dialed into our private little chat room. Maybe she was at her desk. I started typing.

Board Betty, anybody home? I waited.

Hey Tanner, what's happening? You haven't been answering my messages!

All right! She was home.

I know, sorry. I typed the reply as fast as I could. **Blew out my knee. Am in the city for a few weeks for rehab.**

Awesome! she typed. That confused me a little bit.

Thanks a lot. I was trying to sound sarcastic.

No, silly, she continued, **I mean sorry about your knee but we can finally meet I.R.L!**

I.R.L. In real life. I felt my stomach knot up a bit. It would be pretty weird seeing this girl face to face. She probably had some picture of me in her mind and I had no idea what she looked like. I mean, she'd described herself as having short dark hair and blue eyes but that describes a lot of people.

Hello. Anybody there? Another line of print appeared on the screen. I'd been staring at the screen for over a minute.

Cool, I responded, **when and where?**

How about tonight? At Molten Java's, the coffee shop where I work. Woodview and Brighton. My shift is over at eight.

It's a plan. I wrote, clicked send, and then wished I hadn't said something so cheesy.

I found the rehabilitation center without too much problem. It looked just like a gym with all the free weights and resistance-type machines they had. The physiotherapist was expecting me. The first thing she asked me to do was put down my crutches and stand up on both my legs. It was the first time I had tried to stand without my crutches and I held to the side of the hospital bed just in case. It worked. I could stand.

"Hey, this doesn't even hurt," I said. "I could have been walking around before today. Why didn't the doctor tell me?"

The physiotherapist laughed. "You didn't do yourself any harm staying off it for a few days," she answered, "although you'll be surprised at just how much muscle you've lost by not putting any weight on it for a few days. Try and flex your quadriceps and you'll see."

I tightened up all my leg muscles and looked down. She was right. I couldn't believe it. I did a lot of mountain biking and my left leg had a muscle that bulged out above my kneecap. The right one used to as well, but now it looked as if I wasn't even flexing. "How can I have lost muscle so fast?" I asked.

"Muscles shrink, or atrophy as we call it, quickly when you don't use them," she said. "But don't worry. Your quad and your VMO, this muscle on the inside of your knee, will come back really quickly once you start on a program. Give it a month. Be thankful you aren't stuck in a cast for six weeks. Then you'd see some really serious shrinkage!"

"What do you want me to do," I asked, "squats, bike, what?"

"We'll start out slowly," she said. You can't build all that muscle back up in just one day. Today I just want you to do some stretching and bending, and we'll get you to start bearing weight on the leg. Afterwards we'll give you some ultrasound which will help reduce the swelling and promote healing. Have you been icing it regularly?"

I had to admit I hadn't. It's not the most pleasant sensation, but I promised to do it more. I felt relieved to be standing on my own, less like an injured person. I spent the hour trying to bend and straighten my bad knee. I did some reverse squats at a machine that took some of the weight off rather than adding it on. The session ended with some ultrasound, which feels like someone rubbing a microphone across your skin. I couldn't feel a thing. Then more ice. The physiother-apist told me that with some effort on my part, my knee would soon be could be back to normal, in about four weeks.

"How about snowboarding?' I asked.

"Not today," she said.

"No, I know, but when?"

"Well, it's not the worst thing you could do for your knee, but you'll have to be very careful not to fall and re-injure it again. The swelling is going to take a while to go down com-pletely, particularly if you don't ice it. Also, can you stop using both your crutches? Maybe try using just one, or get yourself a cane. Bearing weight on that knee will help bring the mus-cle back more than anything."

"When will it be back to normal?"

"Like I said, all going well, four weeks."

I walked out of that place half walking, half using my crutches and feeling pretty good. I figured I could be back on my board in two weeks, tops.

I had a list of exercises that I had to do twice a day at home in addition to my session at the center. I was doing knee bends on the stairs with a hand on the handrail like some kind of ballet dancer when my dad came home.

"What exactly are you doing?"

"Physio."

"What did they say?"

"Full recovery, two weeks."

CHAPTER 8

I gave myself a lot of time to catch a bus and hobble to the coffee shop, so I got there at ten minutes before eight. I looked at the door and considered walking around the block once or twice to kill some time, but in view of the icy pavement and the fact that I was still on crutches I decided that was stupid. I pushed open the door, walked in, sat down at a table near the window and started scanning the place.

I knew it was her right away. She had short dark hair all right, and it bounced as she cleared coffee cups off a table and carried the tray into the back. She wore a little skirt with tights and boots and had a plaid shirt on. Very cute. A few moments later she came and looked in my direction and smiled. She had a wide white smile that made the corners of her eyes crinkle up and made my stomach flip. She walked over to my table with two cups of coffee on her tray.

"And you must be Tanner."

"How'd you guess?"

"Psychic, I guess," that smile again, "and the crutches are pretty hard to miss. You want some coffee?" I nodded and she put the coffees on the table and sat down. Wow. I'd been an idiot not to have met this girl before now.

"So," I asked her, "how do you find the time to go to school, ride, keep a job and post on the Net? Are you super-organized, or what?"

She rubbed her eyes. "I wish I had a cool answer to that, but I guess I kind of am. I'm also super-tired most of the time, but I don't care. I like my life kind of crazy. My boss is pretty cool, she lets me switch my shifts whenever I have too much work to do for school or whenever there's been a really major dump of snow."

I thought things were going pretty well. She was as easy to talk to in person as in cyberspace.

"Are you snowboarding much these days?"

"Every weekend. When are you going to be able to get back into it?" she asked, eyeing my crutches. "Looks pretty serious."

"It's not so bad. I might be heading back as early as next week. The guys say it's just not the same up there without me," I joked.

"Sounds like the good old days are over for everyone up at Sighing Pass, doesn't it?" Jenny said, taking a sip of her coffee. "What with all that bad press and that corporation trying to take over the place."

I nearly choked on a mouthful of coffee. "What are you talking about?" I spluttered.

"When was the last time you checked out the regional homepage?" she asked. "There's been all kinds of gossip lately about your mountain."

"Gossip?" I still wasn't believing my ears. Was I the last person to know about this? "What gossip? Tell me everything. I haven't touched a computer in two weeks except to e-mail you."

"Well, let me start from the beginning." She frowned, and I found myself being momentarily distracted by how cute that made her look. Her next words, however, jolted me back from my trance.

"I saw it in the newspaper first. There was a story about this corporation, Ski Northwest, that wants to buy the ski resort at Sighing Pass. But there are all kinds of problems with the negotiations, like a lawsuit about allegations that the area has unsafe snowpack."

"Unsafe snowpack? What does that mean?"

She looked up at me. "I wondered the same thing so I posted in the chat room and asked what they meant by it."

"And....did you get an answer?"

"Well, sort of," she replied, frowning in that cute way again. I felt a fluttering feeling in my stomach. "Some rider who goes to the university posted an explanation. It seems that sometimes when there's a warm day, ice crystals form on top of the snow and make a weak layer. Then when more layers of new snow pile up on top, there's still this brittle layer buried beneath that can collapse and then-"

"Avalanche," I finished the sentence for her. "The heavy layers on top crush the weak layer, the snowpack loses its stability, and the whole thing starts to slide."

She nodded. "It's got another name, depth frost or hoar frost or something. But..."

"But what?"

"Well, this is what all the gossip is about. It seems that some places have lots of problems with it, like Colorado, but it's not supposed to be such a problem out here on the coast. I mean, we have avalanches too, but they aren't usually caused by this."

"You learned all this on the Net?"

She smiled. "Physical geography is my favorite subject at school, and I'm doing some independent work for my teacher.

Do you want a warm-up?"

I looked down to see that my coffee had gone cold. "Sure, thanks." She got up to go and get it and I watched her walk away. Very cute, nice, and smart, too. I was a goner.

CHAPTER 9

I waited for the screen to come up. That's the problem with the Internet, it's so damned slow, you wait all day to get where you want to be. Then it appeared. Someone certainly knew their stuff.

Depth hoar, that was the culprit being blamed for Sighing Pass' recent problems. A formation of weak ice crystals and air space deep under the snow, susceptible to collapse under strain or rapid temperature change and likely to cause an avalanche. It didn't make any sense. We'd been riding out of bounds for years. We knew the dangers of snow slides. We wouldn't go if there had been a lot of snowfall, or if it suddenly warmed up. Sometimes we'd dig a pit and jump around on the uphill side of it to see if the pack would hold. People have been skiing at Sighing Pass for ten years and sure, there were slides sometimes, but usually the Ski Patrol would plant dynamite and blow down all the dangerous parts. The risk had always seemed minimal. Never had we had so many avalanches, and certainly not in so many places that the Ski Patrol had checked out. Earlier in the season something happened that was almost unheard of. At night, a sudden avalanche had buried one of the big snow cats used for grooming the slopes. It was a lucky thing that the driver had the sense to use his radio to call for help. The big machine had been rolled down a 100-meter slope and the driver had to be dug out from beneath all the snow. The cat was badly damaged and the poor guy was pretty shaken up. And never before had so many snowboarders been having strange accidents, either.

The two weeks passed slowly. I went to physiotherapy, did my exercises and got fitted for a knee brace. My knee was definitely getting better. I went from not even being able to bend my knee enough to ride the stationary bike to being able to do knee bends standing on my injured leg. And I iced it so often that I got to like the feeling of the wet dishtowel full of ice cubes against my skin. I e-mailed my homework to Mr. Ryerson and talked to Jenny everyday. She wanted to get out for a day of free riding and by Sunday I figured my knee was up to it. My dad didn't agree.

"Tanner, it's a bit soon..."

"I'll take it easy, Dad, I promise," I said, giving him (I hoped) a confidence-inspiring grin. I already had my gear by the front door. He ran a hand through his gray-flecked hair.

"No brain, no pain," he sighed.

I smiled. The buzzer sounded and I pressed the intercom button. "Hello?"

"Hey Tanner, ready to go?"

"I'm on my way down."

I had to congratulate myself on the way to Quail, the local ski area where Jenny usually rode. Being with Jenny, going snowboarding, nice sunny day - it couldn't be better. I leaned back in the seat and prepared myself for an excellent time.

It was a great session. It was only Jenny's second season but she was getting pretty good. She made smooth toe and heel edge turns, and was game to try any trail on the mountain. I wasn't though, with my bad knee, and so we rode the lifts, hit all the easy inbounds stuff, and stopped a lot to drink hot chocolate or just hang out in the sun. It was fun. It reminded me of when I first started snowboarding and was just getting the hang of it. I could barely get down the hill without falling on my face or my butt every two meters but I knew this sport was for me. I got so hooked I free rode all day for the fun of it. That was before I started hanging around the halfpipe and concentrating on doing tricks and harder styling moves.

Jenny was totally cool to be with. I didn't feel nervous anymore at all. We were flirting with each other a lot, and we talked non-stop. She wore a baggy light blue jacket with beige snowboarding pants. With her short dark hair peeking out from under a woolly toque and her bright blue eyes I thought she was one of the prettiest girl I'd ever seen. Lots of the other riders seemed to know her and say hi. It felt great to be with her.

"Hope I'm not holding you back!" she called over her shoulder as we started down a smooth intermediate slope.

"No way," I yelled back. "This is just what the doctor ordered." I winced. I had to stop using those stupid clichés. I sounded like an idiot. "But my knee is starting to ache. You want to go inside for a while?"

"Fine with me."

I felt a little funny leaving my board outside unattended after what happened to it before, but Jenny assured me that snowboarders were pretty welcome at Quail and it would probably be OK. It seemed that every resort except Sighing Pass has realized that snowboarding is a huge money-making phenomenon. Lots of people out here in the mountains started skiing when they were little kids and it doesn't hold the same kind of allure anymore. Everyone skis, it's nothing special. I know kids that go skiing just to spend a little time outdoors with their grandmothers.

Snowboarding, on the other hand, has attitude. The equipment costs about the same as that for skiing, and actually it's a lot easier to learn to snowboard than ski, but there's something about it. You can tell a snowboarder at a glance. They're the ones in the long baggy jackets that keep them dry when they're sitting on the snow, and the mismatched pants that have knee patches for the same reason. You don't see any brightly coordinated ski suits in the halfpipe. Fashions change pretty quickly, but one thing stays the same. There's no way you'd confuse a snowboarder with a skier.

And then there are the moves. Borrowing a little from surfing and a lot from skateboarding, snowboarding takes on the same rebellious attitude those sports have. Add to that the technical difficulty and the guts it takes to master some of the flips and jumps, and you've got the makings of a multi-million-dollar craze.

Most resorts have cashed in on this by building permanent snowboard parks along the line of skateboard parks, with lots of stuff to keep riders happy. They have jumps, courses for boardercross (like a downhill BMX bike race), rails to slide down and of course, the halfpipe. The halfpipe looks exactly as it sounds, a wide, U-shaped chute on a moderate slope. Riders drop in, ride up the opposite wall, flip or turn and drop back in ready to hit the other side. Things get really exciting when riders start taking vertical air right out of the pipe and do a difficult trick, like a 540 rotation, or grab an edge before dropping back in.

"Jenny! Over here!" I looked over to see who was calling her. It was Bucky, one of the old riders from Sighing Pass. He was sitting at a table littered with the remains of a plate of fries. With him were a couple other boarders I vaguely recognized from my high school. We went over and sat down.

"Hey, Tanner, how's it going?" he asked me. "I didn't know you were a friend of our Jenny's."

"Yeah," I said. Our Jenny's? "I thought you were in Colorado."

"Just got back this week. Ran out of cash so I came back here to work."

"You working here at Quail?"

"Bucky's working as a liftie here," explained Jenny.

He nodded. "It's not so bad, y'know. They give me a free lift pass."

"Cool," I said. "So you're coming up for the contest?"

"Sure, man. Wouldn't miss it. There's a couple guys here who can help judge it for ya. They're pretty good." He stood up. "Well, gotta get back to work. Talk to you later, Jenny. See ya, Tanner."

Once he'd gone I turned to Jenny. "I didn't know you two knew each other so well."

She looked at me and then punched me in the shoulder. "You're jealous, aren't you?" she laughed.

"No, just wondering."

"I've been riding with those guys a lot lately. They're really nice."

Yeah, I bet, I thought to myself.

We went out for a few more runs and then called it a day. Jenny let me drive on the way back although I only had my learner's permit. She rubbed the back of my neck with her hand and I could hardly concentrate on the road. We pulled up to my dad's building way too soon.

"No, I've really got to get going," she said in response to my invitation to stay for dinner. "I've got some homework to finish up and then I have a shift at the café."

I shook my head.

"How do you do all the things you do?" I asked her.

She shrugged. "Nervous energy, I guess." Then she leaned over and kissed me on the cheek. "Thanks for coming out."

"I should be thanking you," I said, reaching over and gently turning her face towards mine. "You're pretty amazing, Betty, you know that?" And I kissed her back, but on the lips this time.

CHAPTER 10

My knee was stiff and swollen the next morning and I could barely walk. My dad didn't say anything, he just gave me those "I told you so" looks. I didn't say anything either; I kept the ice pack on it and I told the physiotherapist that I'd probably been walking around too much.

I had the place pretty much to myself. My dad was out at work all day. He was usually out all evening as well, with one of the women who were always calling him. Some of the meetings were for business he told me, but I doubted that. It kind of made me feel a bit sorry for my mom. She hadn't been out with anyone in a long time.

I was keeping up with my schoolwork without too much difficulty. I was in contact with Mr. Ryerson every day by e-mail and he seemed satisfied. And I was turning up all kinds of stuff on the Internet about what was happening at Sighing Pass.

I found some more information about Ski Northwest, the corporation that was trying to acquire the Sighing Pass ski resort. The CEO, Nathan Pride, had taken over two other resorts in the last five years and seemed to buy, at rock bottom prices, places that were having more than their share of troubles.

One ski area had had a sudden rash of equipment failures,

culminating in three gondolas detaching from the overhead cable and plunging down a mountainside. Two people were killed and more than a dozen were injured in the accident. The new owners overhauled or replaced every lift and the resort began to get back on its feet. At the other resort, several top-level managers were charged and convicted of embezzling money from the area operating fund. Once they had been replaced with Ski Northwest personnel, the resort recovered financially and started to show a profit.

Was Sighing Pass becoming as beleaguered as these two resorts had been before their respective take-overs? Maybe so, but it seemed very odd that depth hoar, a natural weakness deep within the snowpack, would suddenly manifest itself in a rash of accidents in a single year.

I was puzzling over this one evening when the phone rang. It was my mom.

"Tanner." Her voice sounded all tight and funny. "I've got some bad news for you. I'm so sorry."

I suddenly felt cold. "Is it Connor? Are the dogs all right?"

"The dogs are fine, they're right here. It's Jonas, darling. There's been an accident, an avalanche."

"What do you mean?" My throat felt like it was being squeezed and my voice was coming out in little bursts. "What happened? Is he OK?"

"Sweetheart." Mom sounded like she was crying. "He was completely buried. No one saw it happen. He had a beacon on and they found him as soon as they realized he was missing but it was too late-"

"No!" I shouted. "I don't believe it." I was crying now too. A million thoughts were going through my mind. Jonas showing off on a kicker, laughing at school, hanging out at the shop.

He couldn't be just gone, just erased, just like that. It wasn't possible. It couldn't be true.

"Tanner, are you still there?"

"Yes."

"Do you want me to come and get you? I think some people here need you. Can you come? Is your knee well enough?"

"Yeah, Mom. Can you come right away?" I asked. I felt like a little kid.

"I'm on my way," she replied. "I'm so sorry, Tanner. I'll be there soon."

I hung up and stared at the white wall of my Dad's study. *A white wall, that must have been the last thing that Jonas saw...*

CHAPTER 11

"I can't believe it, I just can't," said Trevor, rubbing his eyes. "It's just not like Jonas to go off into a couloir alone like that, not following anybody, or anyone's tracks."

All the members of the SOS were in the back of Mike's shop talking about what had happened. We'd all been to the funeral that morning and no one felt like being alone afterwards. Mike had closed the shop for the day and we were all sitting around wearing unfamiliar shirts and ties. I felt like I was choking, but when I took my tie off I didn't feel any better.

"They are saying, you know, it is because of this depth hoar," said Xavier. "My father thinks this is crazy. There should not be so many slopes avalanching like this. We have sometimes this problem in France but *ici, ce n'est pas possible.*"

"Jonas wasn't a kamikaze dude," said Mike, passing around mugs of coffee. "In my opinion he had the best judgment out of bounds of any of you. He would never have dropped into anything that was sketchy unless he was following someone he trusted or first tracks had already been laid. Excuse me, guys," he said, putting a pair of the new wide powder skis in the vice, "I just need to be doing something right now and I told that new patroller I'd have these skis ready for him."

I wrapped my hands around my mug of coffee and thought about Jonas. It still didn't make any sense, no one thought so. I had a feeling in my stomach that something else was up. Something big. All these strange accidents couldn't be mere coincidences. Maybe someone was out to get snow-boarders.

I shut my eyes and tried to think. So maybe it didn't happen the way we thought after all. Of course Jonas wouldn't have made any of those mistakes. He didn't make any of those mistakes. Either he got an expert's opinion on the snow conditions, or he followed someone he trusted in and the slope gave way. My throat tightened some more. Because whoever it had been hadn't stuck around to dig Jonas out. Whose judgment would Jonas have trusted completely? Certainly not another rider. Who then? I opened my eyes and they came to rest on the skis that Mike was waxing. I barely heard Trevor saying something about dedicating this year's Out of Bounds contest to Jonas' memory. I excused myself. I had to get out of there, had to figure this out. For Jonas..

When I got home I tossed on some real clothes, called the dogs, and headed up the ridge path. Our chalet is on the side of the valley and pretty high up. It's only a short walk to the end of the road and up a short steep gully to a rock ridge that overlooks the west side of the resort.

Sherpa abruptly angled off into the bush. The dogs were always doing that; they'd pick up the scent of a small animal, rabbit, squirrel or marmot and suddenly the wild side of their nature would kick in. They'd follow that scent, oblivious to voices commanding them to come back. But they aren't wild animals and Mom and I would never really worry because soon enough they'd come barreling back to us, nearly knocking us over in their haste to be with us again.

Sometimes I could see or hear what it was they were after, but not usually. Winter, though, made it easier for humans, whose senses were dulled from ages of being "civilized." I could read stories in the snow about what was happening in the woods. Once, Mom and I saw a set of tiny mouse tracks ending between two fanned out marks like a miniature snow angel, and in the center, a smear of blood. Mom had asked me to figure out what had happened and I pieced it together. A hungry owl had swooped down and made a meal out of the tiny animal.

My knee felt pretty strong as I floundered up through the fresh soft snow. I couldn't quite straighten it all the way, so I swung the whole thing forward as a unit to step instead of kicking out the foot. I had a bit of trouble on the steepest part of the gully, but I grabbed hold of Connor's collar and he bounded up, half dragging me. Once on top I flopped down in the snow to rest. The dogs sniffed around. I felt warm, even overheated, in my snowboarding clothes and I pulled off my toque. I had a great view of the resort from this spot.

I watched as a skier swooped in graceful turns down the mountain and then plunged off the side of the groomed run onto a section of clean, untouched, powder snow, the rhythm of his turns never faltering. "He's pretty good," I thought to myself. "It's not often you see such smooth skiing." Coming onto the packed groomed surface again, he tucked his body in a tight racing crouch and accelerated out of sight. He'd been using a pair of those new fat powder skis, probably the reason behind those perfect powder turns. In his wake he'd left shiny S-shaped tracks that glistened silver in the late afternoon light. Suddenly I shivered.

Tracks.

It must have been tracks that Jonas had followed. Tracks that led to a fantastic powder run that he just couldn't resist. Tracks that led to a trap.

CHAPTER 12

School on Tuesday was a mess. Everyone was just standing around in groups, looking sad. A lot of the girls were crying and so were some of the teachers. Jonas' locker looked
like a shrine. There were flowers and pictures cut out of snowboard magazines and cards taped all over it. One card read:
The Soul Surfer. The caretakers left it alone all day, even
though there was stuff all over the floor in front of it. I could-
n't stay there long. I just couldn't take it.

In the morning, our teacher announced that the school
was bringing in grief counselors to help the kids deal with
Jonas' death. Anyone who wanted to talk to them could make
an appointment, anytime. I didn't see how talking to someone
who never even knew Jonas would help. If I felt like talking
about him, I had the rest of the Surfers for that. But I didn't feel
like talking. I felt like doing something - anything - to, I don't
know, even the score somehow. Make things right. Even
though I knew it wouldn't bring Jonas back.

In the afternoon there was a memorial service in the gym.
It was a pretty nice thing, I guess, with teachers and classmates
of Jonas getting up in front of everyone and telling little stories
about him. It ended with a speech by a visitor who was an
avalanche expert. He started by saying he never had the

chance to meet Jonas, but that he did have the chance to meet the rest of us, and maybe have the opportunity to prevent someone else from being killed in an avalanche. I didn't think it was too appropriate, but I guess the point was to make a serious impact on all the kids in the school who probably wouldn't think twice about heading out of bounds to snag first tracks on some manky slope.

I picked up the pamphlet and looked at it. They were offering an avalanche education course that would teach you how to figure out if a slope was safe. In the back of my mind I was thinking about the contest. We were pretty much responsible for making sure that wherever we held it the snow was safe. There would be a lot of riders coming. I put the pamphlet in my backpack.

Brent, the Ski Patroller, was sitting on our couch drinking hot chocolate with my mom when I walked in the door.

"Hello, Tanner," said Brent. "How are you doing?"

I shrugged. "OK, I guess."

My mom got up and walked into the kitchen. "I'll get you some hot chocolate, Tanner, and then we'd like to talk with you for a minute. We're both concerned."

I shrugged, and went to hang up my jacket. When I came back my mom handed me a steaming mug. I sat down.

"We're both really concerned about you and your friends' safety," she began.

"It's not that I don't trust your judgment," interjected Brent. "You've proved yourself in the past. But I trusted Jonas' judgment too, and now..."

I said nothing.

"We just want you to be more careful, now. No riding out of bounds at all. No kickers, no contests. And I have some more bad news."

"What?" I asked.

"I heard that Area Management is planning to ban snowboarding at Sighing Pass. You may not be riding there at all anymore if there are any more incidents involving snowboarders."

I was astonished. "You've got to be kidding!"

"I'm surprised, too," said Brent. "I think it's a knee-jerk reaction to what has happened. I also think they're under a lot of pressure to sell the place and they're trying to get the best price they can. The value of this resort is going down fast. They're coming down hard on the Ski Patrol, too. No one is immune from this."

"What have you guys done?"

"It's what we haven't done. We've had more post-control slides this year than ever before."

"What are post-control slides?" asked my mom.

"They're snow slides that happen after we've controlled the slope for avalanches. We usually traverse diagonally across it with skis to minimize the risk, or we use explosives to bring down all the unstable snow. Now, not all avalanche control work is 100 percent effective, there's always some risk, but too many slopes have come down when they shouldn't. We're really under fire. Not that we have enough people or resources to patrol a resort of this size." I was surprised at the bitterness in his voice.

"I don't want any more accidents to happen to you or your friends," Mom said to me. "So just take it easy, OK? No risky stuff."

"No, I know, Mom." It was easiest just to agree with her. "In fact, I picked this up today." I handed her the avalanche pamphlet. "We're thinking of going." Mom flipped through it.

"Not a bad idea," she said. "When is it? Next week some-time?"

"Yeah, every night next week."

Mom started nodding her head. She likes it when there is some action she can take to solve a problem. "You should go. I'll give you the money. Are your other friends going?"

"Yeah, I think so," I said. "Any calls for me?"

"Jenny called. She'd like you to call her back."

"OK. Can I go now?" She nodded. I walked down the hall to my room feeling even more depressed after hearing that, as usual, snowboarders were catching all the blame. Was there no end to all this? I picked up the phone and dialed Jenny's number.

She sounded a little shy on the phone.

"I'm so sorry, Tanner. I just read about it in the paper. I called your dad's but he said you'd gone back to Sighing Pass. When was the funeral?"

"Yesterday. It was awful."

"I feel terrible for you. I wish I could be there."

"Thanks."

"Is there anything I can do?'

"You're doing it. Just keep talking. Tell me about something else."

"Well, I was thinking about how much I miss you."

"Yeah, and?"

"And I was thinking that I could drive up this weekend and see you. That is, if you're in the mood for company."

I took a deep breath. "That would be great," I said. "Your parents will let you take the car?"

"Yeah. I already checked it out with them. I just need a

place to stay."

"You can stay here if you want."

"I was hoping you'd say that. It's fine with my parents as long as your mother is there."

"She's here now. Do they want to speak to her?"

"Yeah. Is that all right?"

"Sure."

CHAPTER 13

After school on Friday, the three remaining Surfers were hanging out at Xav's, fooling around on the kicker. We were all still totally bummed. The others were doing some half-hearted jumps off the lip. I didn't trust my knee yet, so I was sitting on the picnic table watching. Trevor was trying his new board for the first time. Sitting there, watching Xav's board carve tracks in the snow as he landed off the jump, I was reminded of what I had seen from the top of the ridge.

"Hey, Trevor, come here a sec."

"What?" He slid up to the bench and sat down.

"Trevor, that day that your board got trashed-"

"Never forget it," he grumbled. "Jerks."

"Yeah. What were you doing before it happened?"

"Uhh. Oh, yeah. I'd been in the chalet chilling out - Xav and I'd just hiked back from the saddle and we were beat."

"What were you doing out there?"

"Checking it out as a site for the contest."

"Why didn't you ride it down?"

He shrugged. "Slope looked sketchy to me after that storm. We wouldn't even have gone over in the first place if there hadn't already been tracks."

It both shocked and didn't shock me at the same time.

"Tracks? Whose?"

"'Dunno," he answered. "Some skier with the new wide skis. They didn't ski down either, though. Tracks headed back the same way."

I wanted to tell him that I thought something sinister was happening at Sighing Pass, but there were still a few pieces missing from the puzzle. Someone was doing something out of bounds to sabotage the resort, and didn't want anyone to find out. And who were the only other people out of bounds all the time who could see them? Snowboarders, that's who. Snowboarders could figure out what they were doing and ruin the whole thing. Whoever was responsible would do anything to scare the boarders off. But I still couldn't figure out what it was that they could be doing out there. And I didn't believe anyone would go as far as murdering kids to keep a secret. I knew that stories could be written in snow and that tracks could not always be covered. Unusual tracks. Tracks made by someone skiing on the new wide powder skis.

It felt like a snowball had suddenly hit me in the face. The Ski Patrol! Of course! The avalanche technicians whose duty it was to search out and eliminate the danger of any unsafe slope would be the only people whose tracks Jonas would have followed. Some of them used wide skis, like Jeff, the new guy who'd given me a hard time when I hurt my knee. A million new questions flooded my mind. Why would a patroller, responsible for rescuing people, lure someone into danger? How could they trigger an avalanche, yet avoid being swept away themselves? And why?

"You know, I hate this," Trevor was saying. I hadn't been listening.

"You hate what?' I asked.

"Jonas being gone. I don't feel like doing anything. Not school, not listening to music, not even that." He gestured towards Xav, who had just landed a jump off the kicker.

"Yeah, I know what you mean."

Xav undid one binding and shuffled over to where Trevor and I were sitting.

"You guys aren't into riding today, are you?" he asked. Trevor and I both just kind of looked at him. "It's Jonas, isn't it?"

Trevor threw a snowball at the side of the house, hard. "An accident like that just shouldn't happen."

Xavier loosened his other binding and sat down on the picnic table. "It does, though. Accidents do happen. In the mountains, people can get killed."

"Not around here they don't," I said.

"That's true," he agreed. "But in the mountains in France, it did happen sometimes."

"To any of your friends?" I asked.

Xav picked his jacket up off the table and put it on. "I remember one time very well," he said. "It made me understand for the first time what the mountains are like. It has happened to my father many times. He was a guide and spent lots of time in the mountains before he learned to fly a helicopter. Anyway, there was a boy I knew at school. His name was Jacques. He wasn't a friend of mine because he was a few years older than I was. He was very good at skiing and snowboarding. He was popular at school because he could go down the steepest mountainside and he went over jumps that we were, you know, afraid to do. He was also a good mountaineer and he wanted to become a guide, like my father. He would come to our house and talk to my father sometimes."

"What happened to him?" asked Trevor.

"He was snowboarding one day by himself and he was going to meet some friends afterwards. He didn't show up. No one was worried at first because he knew the mountains so well and the weather was good. There hadn't been any avalanches or anything like that. Sometimes he would take a sleeping bag and a bivouac sack, you know what I mean?" We nodded. A bivouac sack is sort of like a tent for one. It's a water-resistant bag that you put your sleeping bag inside and crawl into. It doesn't have poles or anything, but it's better than nothing and it's light and easy to carry. "He would stay out overnight in the mountains by himself.

"By the next day everyone in the town was very worried. His parents told us that all his camping equipment was still at their house. They had called all his friends and no one had seen him. So my father organized a search for him. Each search team had some guides and some kids on it because we knew were he liked to ride. We spent all day looking for him in the steep couloirs and the places off-piste where he used to go a lot."

"Did you find him?"

Xav zipped his jacket up higher and shook his head. "Not that day," he said. "We checked every place we could think of. I was so tired because we climbed very high on the mountain. All the climbers from the town were out looking, too. We had radios and we talked with each other but there was no sign of him."

"What happened to him?"

"It was so stupid," he said. "My team, we found him the next day. We hadn't even started looking yet, we were coming to rendezvous with the others. One of my friends saw his jacket in the snow and we found him. He was very close to the town, up the side of the valley in the trees. He must have been taking a short-cut down through the trees, probably to meet his friends. It's something we all did, all the time. But there was a lot of snow and around each tree, you know how the snow is very soft and there is like a hole?"

"You mean a tree well?" asked Trevor.

"*Oui*. He had fallen in a tree well by himself and maybe hurt himself just a little bit. But he could not take his snowboard off, you know? It was buried and he couldn't reach it or something, I don't know. Anyway it was very cold and he couldn't get out and I guess no one could hear him."

"And he froze?" I finished.

Xav nodded. "It was terrible," he said. "No one could understand why he couldn't get out. And he was so close to the town. He didn't crash into a rock or get caught in an avalanche or have a big accident like that, he was just taking a short-cut through the trees. The very same short-cut my search team was taking." Xav took off his glasses and used his hat to clean some snow off them. "After that I didn't want to go out in the mountains like I did before. I was afraid. If an accident could happen to someone like Jacques, who was so good at everything, then it could happen to me, too."

I nodded. I kind of felt like that, too. "But you go out there everyday, Xav!"

"I know, now I do. My father talked to me. He told me that you can't control everything that might happen in the mountains. You can learn a lot but sometimes you can make a mistake or have bad luck. Maybe Jacques would be OK if he was not alone that day. But maybe he just had some bad luck. It's not that the mountains are bad. They are only mountains. I started to listen to my father to learn more about the mountains. He took me out on a trip right after it happened. It was a beautiful trip. We tried something difficult. We climbed part of the Petit Dru. Do you know it?" I didn't. "No? It's a mountain near Chamonix. It's very beautiful. We climbed very high and I wanted to go higher. But my father thought a storm was coming and we turned back."

"Did you get caught in the storm?" asked Trevor.

"No. The storm passed by. We could have climbed higher. But my father was right. If we were caught in the storm up there it would have been very dangerous. So now, I do go out into the mountains, but I try to learn about the weather and the snow and if I think it is dangerous I turn around. It is stupid otherwise. But it is also stupid not to go into the mountains at all."

"I think you're right," Trevor said. "Jonas wouldn't have wanted us to stop snowboarding because of what's happened. Snowboarding meant everything to him."

"Somehow I can't believe that it was an accident," I said. The guys looked at me. "It just seems too weird, you know?" They nodded.

Xav picked up his board and scraped some snow off of it with his glove. "I have an idea. My father is feeling very bad about Jonas and he wants to do something to put us into a good humor. I told him that we are OK, but he insists. He wants to take us up in the helicopter, over past the saddle and for us to go riding out there together. I told him I would ask you. What do you think?"

I squinted up at him. "That's really nice of your dad," I said. "Sure, I'd be into it. Oh, wait. Jenny's coming up tonight to visit for the weekend. I can't."

"It's OK, there are enough seats in the helicopter for

another person. She can come too. How about you, Trevor?"

Trevor shrugged. "Sure, I'm in. Anything to get me out of this funk."

"OK, it is settled. I will tell my father that we will go with him tomorrow morning, early."

CHAPTER 14

It would be my first time flying in a helicopter, but I didn't feel very excited about it that evening. I could tell my mom wasn't too pleased about the idea either, although she said she did trust Xavier's dad, Mr. Dupuis, as an expert helicopter guide. She called up Brent and I could hear her asking him what he thought of it. He must have reassured her somehow, as she seemed a little more relaxed after that and didn't argue with me anymore. I wandered around the house for a while wondering when Jenny would get there. Finally, headlights appeared at the bottom of the drive.

The first thing she did when she came inside was give me a hug, which kind of startled me since my mom was right there. They seemed to hit it off right away, though, and Mom took her upstairs to show her the room she'd be staying in. Right next to her own, of course. While Jenny was unpacking her things, I told her everything about what I thought was happening at Sighing Pass.

"Sounds like a movie-of-the-week."

"I'm serious, Jenny, it's more than just coincidence. Someone has to stop what's going on."

"No, I didn't mean it that way, Tanner. It's just that it's so crazy-sounding. Who's going to believe a story like that coming from a sixteen-year-old snowboarder?"

"I know, I know. I'll just have to find a way to expose whoever is responsible."

"Well, for this weekend, let's just have fun. Try to get your mind off Jonas' accident just for a little while. I can't wait to ride this mountain I've been hearing about for the last year."

"You're going to ride a lot more of it than most people ever do."

"Why's that?"

I told her about the helicopter trip.

"No way!"

"Yeah."

"You don't seem too psyched."

"No, no, I am. I just keep thinking about Jonas all the time. It's pretty hard to get excited about anything."

"I know," she said, and put her arms around my neck. "It will take a long time, you know, before you start to feel better."

"Yeah, I guess. I'm glad you're here." I leaned down and kissed her.

"Tanner! Jenny!" Mom's voice came from downstairs. "You kids want something to eat?" Jenny broke off the embrace and stepped back with a wry smile.

"Guess we better go downstairs," she said.

The next morning dawned clear, cold and sunny. When I got up, Jenny was already in the kitchen drinking coffee with my mom.

"Good morning, Tanner." She smiled and her eyes crinkled up at the edges. She was wearing the same outfit she'd worn on that day at Quail. She really was as pretty as I had remembered.

"Hi, ready to go?"

"Yep, just having some java."

"Do you want some, Tanner?" my mom asked. "Jenny brought us some gourmet coffee beans from the coffee shop."

"Sure." I sat down at the table for some cereal, too.

"Where exactly are you kids headed? Do you know?"

"I think Mr. Dupuis is going to take us up past the saddle. There are some really nice back bowls up in that area."

"What about the snow conditions?"

"It's stayed cold over the last few days, and there hasn't been any new snow. I think it's fine, but Mr. Dupuis will know for sure."

My mom ran a hand through her hair. "I do trust his judgment. I can't help worrying, although I think you all need to do something like this."

"Mom," I admonished her. "It'll be fine. Stop worrying so much."

We drove Jenny's car over to the Alpine Air heliport. Trevor and Xavier were waiting for us. I introduced Jenny to them. Trevor shot me a glance of approval.

"My father is just checking some things," said Xav. "But the helicopter is ready to go." I looked over at the sleek red machine and felt a rush of excitement. A chance of a lifetime! Then I suddenly felt a pang of guilt. Jonas would have loved this. But he wouldn't be, would never be, coming along with us again. Just then Mr. Dupuis returned wearing a flight suit and carrying a clipboard.

"Good morning," he said. "All systems go. Put the snowboards on the rack and climb in. There should be enough headphones for everyone."

We headed out across the tarmac and stashed our boards in two external racks fitted near the helicopter's skids. There was room for five passengers. Jenny snuggled in beside me and squeezed my hand.

We strapped ourselves in and put on our headphones. Mr. Dupuis secured the snowboard racks and climbed into the pilot's seat. Xav sat next to him.

"Can everyone hear me?" His voice came through the headphones. We all gave him the thumbs-up signal. "We're going to take off and try to find a landing place beyond the saddle, maybe at the top of Black Peak. If it is looking good, you will ride down and I will pick you up down on the plateau." Nods and thumbs-up signals all around.

He turned back to the controls and the big main rotor overhead started turning, faster and faster. I barely felt the machine lift off, but the next moment we were skimming over treetops and frozen meadows towards the big peaks. Jenny squeezed my hand again. It was an amazing feeling watching the land scroll by below us. I saw cliff bands fall away to reveal frozen rivers and waterfalls, and then we soared upwards over pristine snow slopes and rocky outcrops. Jenny tapped me on the shoulder and pointed out the window. I looked in the direction she indicated. A mountain goat stood on a rocky ledge, as unlikely and lonely a place for an animal as I had ever seen.

The black volcanic summit of Black Peak came into view. Just below it was a flat plateau of snow. Mr. Dupuis brought the helicopter down low and hovered over it. Snow whipped around us in a cloud.

"Looks OK," he said. The helicopter settled onto its perch and the rotors wound down to a stop. I was so excited I fumbled trying to undo my seat belt. The others were out of the machine ahead of me and had already retrieved their boards. Mr. Dupuis climbed out of the cockpit with his clipboard and topographic map. He consulted it for a moment then pointed down a moderate, untracked slope to a distant plateau.

"That's where I will be waiting," he said. "Have fun." Then he unloaded some rescue packs from the helicopter and handed them around for all of us to wear. He told us they contained avalanche probes, shovels, and first aid supplies. In addition, we were all wearing beacons and were reminded to turned them on. These small radios transmit a constant signal on a certain frequency and could also receive a signal. If one of us were to be lost or buried, the receivers would pick up the signal and help indicate to rescuers where to dig. The only problem was, if some of us were to get buried, the others would have to move pretty fast to dig them out safely. It only takes about three minutes of oxygen deprivation to cause brain damage, and death occurs after about five minutes. When you hear about dogs being brought in to look for buried people, it's usually dead bodies they find.

This day, though, conditions were good and the risk was minimal. The avalanche transceivers were only a precaution. Jenny looked at me with wide blue eyes.

"I'm a little nervous," she confided. I gave her a quick kiss on the nose.

"You'll do fine," I assured her. "Just relax and ride the same way you do at Quail." She nodded. I heard a whoop from Trevor behind me and turned to see him disappear over the edge of the plateau. Xav was next and Jenny and I followed suit.

Heli-boarding was all it's cracked up to be, and more. We ripped that bowl up like it was a piece of paper. In front of me, fine snow kicked up behind Xav and Trevor like vapor trails behind a jet. I buried a rail and swung into a big turn, looking back up the slope to see Jenny swooping down behind me. I could hear the sound of the rotor blades as the red helicopter passed overhead and I saw it settle on the plateau way ahead, like a drop of blood on the snow.

Too soon the run was over and we were laughing and slapping each other on the back and piling our boards into the racks.

"Time enough for one more run, I think," said Mr. Dupuis. "We can stop lower down and you can ride to the chalet."

We all agreed this was a great idea and piled back into the helicopter. Soon familiar features came into view, and when Mr. Dupuis put the whirlybird down near the saddle we all got out. We weren't the first here; I could see tracks traversing the slope above.

"I think perhaps you are wanting to try this out," he said with raised eyebrows. I wondered if Xav had been talking a little too much about the upcoming contest. "The conditions are good today, it's been controlled," he continued. "Now, I must get back to my paying customers." I wandered over to scout out a good line down to the bottom.

I heard the muffled boom and a rumbling somewhere but I thought it was a jet or something. Jenny was the first to realize what was happening. She screamed and pointed up. We all looked. To my horror, the view of the top was obscured by a raging tide of snow heading our way...AVALANCHE!

"*Mon Dieu*!" yelled Mr. Dupuis. "Get in the helicopter! Quick!"

Trevor and Xav dove for the open doors and scrambled across to make room. Mr. Dupuis clambered into the cockpit and started the rotors. Slowly they began to turn. I struggled desperately through the deep snow towards them.

"Tanner! Help!" cried Jenny. She could get no traction with her snowboarding boots on the ice-covered skids. Trevor was attempting to haul her into the helicopter by her arms.

Trying to stay low beneath the now fully-spinning rotor blades, I grabbed her by the hips and boosted her up. She went sprawling into the machine just as the skids of the helicopter left the ground.

"Tanner! Hurry! Get in!" she shrieked. She and Trevor were leaning out, arms outstretched.

"He can't hold it, Tanner! Hurry!" yelled Trevor. Chunks of ice started to pelt down on me. I made a lunge for the open door and the safety of the helicopter.

But it was too late.

CHAPTER 15

Jenny told me later that she had thought that was the end of me, and that it felt like her heart had stopped beating. Trevor said he'd braced himself for the impact of the avalanche against the helicopter. It was that close.

I had pushed off the ground as hard as I could, but as I did I felt my bad knee buckle. My gloved hands briefly gripped the bottom edge of the door opening, and slipped off. What saved me was the helicopter skid, which hooked under my right elbow. Reflexively, I had wrapped my other arm around it in a kind of bear hug, and then, as the helicopter took off, bucking and swaying in the sudden turbulence, I swung my legs up and wrapped them around it, too. Jenny saw what had happened and Mr. Dupuis' quick reaction saved our lives. We lifted up about 20 or 30 meters into the air and quickly traversed 200 meters over the saddle and out of the avalanche's path. The helicopter was seriously tilted to one side. Jenny was still leaning out and looking down and I could see her lips moving. Fully aware of how precarious my position was, I shut my eyes.

Faintly, amid the roar of the rotors, I heard her voice. She was shouting my name. I opened my eyes and looked up.

"Drop! Drop! It's OK!" she yelled, over and over. She had to repeat it several times for me to understand. I turned my head and looked back over my shoulder. I was only about two meters off the ground and the landing looked soft. I swung my legs back down and let go.

I landed in soft deep snow and just lay there, watching the helicopter recede from view. I heard the sound of the rotors get quieter. I took stock of how my body felt. My knee was hurting but I could still bend it. My right elbow was sore from the jerk the skid had inflicted on it and my face felt numb. I didn't feel like moving, so I didn't.

"You're alive, it's OK," I told myself over and over, "you're alive."

* * *

Jenny was the first person to reach me. She was out of breath. She dropped to her knees beside me. "Tanner! Thank God you're all right," she said, in between gasps for air.

"Wow," was all I could say. Soon other faces appeared in my field of vision.

"Can you sit up, dude?" asked Trevor. I accepted his help and groggily rose to a sitting position. Xavier was there too, looking concerned.

"The helicopter is not far away," he said. "Can you manage it?"

I nodded. He and Trevor helped me stand up. I could see the helicopter where it had landed, some distance below us. My friends had climbed up to reach me.

"I'm OK," I finally managed to speak. "Let's get out of here." We helped one another wade slowly down through the snow to the waiting helicopter.

The flight back to the heliport was subdued. I think everyone must have been in shock. Looking back into the bowl I could see the pile of debris that had been the slope.

Huge ice chunks and slabs of snow were piled on top of one another at the bottom. Had one of us been swept down in it he would have been crushed. Or she. Mr. Dupuis was on the radio most of the way back, reporting the major slide that had nearly wiped us out. Jenny held tightly onto my hand the whole way back to the heliport.

Mr. Dupuis was shocked and furious. His French accent sounded very strong as he explained the incident over and over on the phone to Area Management. It was the same story all over again. The slope had been controlled. It should have been stable. Conditions had been consistently cold, no recent dumps of snow and nor was the slope in the 30 to 45 degree range that was prone to slab slides. Another freak avalanche in Sighing Pass. His voice was getting louder and louder, insisting all the while that never in his entire career as a mountain guide had such an incident occurred. I knew what was happening on the other end of that phone line. Mr. Dupuis was listening to the sound of Area Management panicking as they saw the value of the resort plummet even further. They were trying to place the blame on someone else, anyone else.

After a while, Jenny felt ready to drive home from the heliport. We'd already called my mom and she was waiting by the door for us. She hugged Jenny and then me. Both of us submitted to her fussing over us; she insisted on hot baths, dry clothes, and then hot chocolate in front of the fire. I turned on the TV and we were idly flipping through the channels when an image of Sighing Pass caught my eye.

"There it is!" Jenny sat up suddenly and elbowed me in the ribs.

"Another near miss adds to the troubles at Sighing Pass Ski Resort," the announcer was saying. "Earlier today, a commercial helicopter operator and his young passengers narrowly escaped tragedy when an avalanche was suddenly triggered above where the group was unloading their gear. They had believed the slope to be stable and safe. The pilot managed to take off and fly all of his passengers out of the path of the oncoming avalanche. This is only the latest occurrence in a series of unusual accidents at the Sighing Pass Ski Resort. It closely follows the death of a young snowboarder in an avalanche last week. Our reporter spoke to Sighing Pass Area Manager, Mr. Karl Sorenson."

The next image filling the television screen was the front of the Sighing Pass chalet. It was crowded with skiers. Mr. Sorenson stood facing the camera, dressed in a red ski suit. A reporter stuck a microphone in his face.

"Do you have any comment about the recent accidents?" asked the reporter. Mr. Sorenson smiled into the camera.

"Sighing Pass has always upheld some of the toughest safety standards in the country," he said. "This season has been very strange in the sense that there has been unusual and unsettled weather patterns in this part of the province, as well as some freak occurrences here at Sighing Pass. At this point, we don't believe this latest incident is anything more than a tragic coincidence. We continually review our safety practices and maintain that our area is one of the safest in the industry."

"So, you believe the skiing at Sighing Pass is safe?" the reporter asked.

Mr. Sorenson smiled at the camera. "Safer than driving a car."

"Is it true that Sighing Pass may be forced to close because of the rising cost of insurance?"

Mr. Sorenson's smile never faltered as he denied that concern. The news broadcast turned to other topics and I turned off the TV

"That poor man," said Jenny, "seeing all he's worked for collapse just like that."

"Yeah," I said. "I wonder if there is some way we can prove that it's really sabotage."

"What happened today, do you think that was part of it?"

"Sure, you saw them too, didn't you?" I asked her.

"The tracks?"

"Yes."

"Yeah, I did see them. Your crazy theory is getting more and more convincing. But there is one thing I do know for sure."

"What's that?"

She snuggled closer to me on the couch.

"You saved my life today."

CHAPTER 16

Jenny left for the city early Sunday morning. My mom and I were still pretty stunned about the whole thing and we both wandered around the house doing a lot of nothing. Actually, everyone involved was shocked and confused. Brent came over again in the afternoon. He and my mom hugged one another and he called her by her nickname, Sally. Only a few of her friends call her that. Everyone else calls her Sarah. I suddenly realized that Brent had been around a lot lately, and he and my mom seemed very comfortable with one another. It made me feel kind of funny. My dad had had plenty of girlfriends since the divorce and I was used to that idea, but my mom... Was there something going on between her and Brent? He seemed too old for her. His hair was completely gray and his face was lined from spending a lot of time outdoors. Something about his blue eyes made all the kids listen to him. He treated snowboarders fairly at the resort, much more so than any of the other patrollers. Everyone respected him.

At dinner I told him about the newscast I had seen.

"We really took a beating from Area Management and the Heli-Ski Operators' Association," he said.

"How come?"

"Mr. Dupuis claimed that the slope above the helicopter

had clearly been controlled. It was on his computer report in the morning."

"Had it?"

Brent sighed. "We couldn't be sure. I put it on our work order for the day and it should have been done by the time you folks landed there. But the risk of avalanche was still really low and it wasn't one of our top priorities. The patroller assigned had been held up with a first aid situation and hadn't had the chance to reassess the slope. It could have been a computer mistake."

Immediately, my suspicions about Jeff came to mind, but something prevented me from asking Brent about him.

"What's happening with Area Management?" I asked instead.

"They're in a tough position. Their resort is becoming associated in people's minds with accidents and danger. Their public image is really suffering and so is their market value. They were worried before about making a profit, and then they were worried about getting a decent price for the place. Now they've seen the value plummet, and the insurance premiums they're required to pay have soared. They're hoping to get out of this mess without losing everything. Everyone involved with Sighing Pass these days has been made to look like a fool, including the Ski Patrol. I wouldn't be surprised if we all found ourselves looking for new jobs next year."

"Wow!" I said. "I didn't know so many people were affected by this."

"And it's not just the people directly involved with running the resort," he continued. "A lot of things would stand to change if the resort went under. Local businesses have enjoyed special agreements with Area Management. They buy food and equipment from people here in town instead of from the city, although that would be cheaper. It helps support the town. If and when Ski Northwest takes over, those agreements may not continue. They might truck in cheaper goods from the city which would be better for them-"

"But not so good for businesses here in town," I finished for him.

"That's right. I don't think this town really understands the impact this take-over is going to have when it happens."

If, I thought to myself. *If* this take-over happens. I knew how Ski Northwest did business; by systematically destroying a place, then dramatically rescuing it at the last moment. Well, they wouldn't succeed this time, not if I had anything to do with it!

I just had to do something. I checked my watch. It was two o'clock, which meant on a Sunday that the resort was in full operation. Everyone in Area Management would be in their offices at the resort. This was my chance! I could make a real difference. I had all the clues I needed to convince anyone that Sighing Pass was being systematically sabotaged. How could they not believe me?

On the way to the resort I went over in my head exactly what I was going to say to Mr. Sorenson. I was going to tell him what I had found out about depth hoar, that it couldn't be responsible for all of the accidents. I was going to tell him why I thought Jonas' death was so suspicious. I would also explain about the little incidents that had been happening among the snowboarders and why we thought someone was trying to keep boarders out of the backcountry where their activities could be seen.

It felt weird to be at the resort in street clothes and not

boarding gear. I went up the stairs and into the chalet. I passed by the snack bar, where a bunch of riders I knew were sitting around. I didn't stop to chat, but I could hear their reaction to my presence.

"Look, there's Tanner! He was the one that nearly got killed in that helicopter yesterday."

"Hey, Tanner! What happened, man?"

"Dude! You guys' OK?"

I waved at them as I cruised on by, and found the stairs leading to the upstairs office. Then I slowed down. This was a part of the resort I'd never been in. I felt like I was trespassing. Maybe this wasn't such a great idea. What if no one believed me? C'mon! I told myself. You have to do this.

I walked down the hallway. There were name plates on each door. I stopped at the one that read KARL SORENSON, AREA MANAGER. I knocked on the closed door, and a voice came from inside.

"Who is it? I'm busy!" I took a deep breath and pushed the door open.

Mr. Sorenson, recognizable to me from his television appearance, looked up from his desk.

"What do you think you're doing in here?" he asked curtly.

"Mr. Sorenson," I began. "I think I know what's causing all these problems at the resort."

"Look, kid. I'm really busy." He stood up at his desk. "If you're looking for a job, go to personnel, it's down the hall."

"I'm not looking for a job," I said. "I think I know what's been happening around here. It's not coincidence. Please, I have a theory..."

He started walking towards me. His eyes narrowed. "Wait a second. Aren't you one of those local snowboarders?"

I nodded with relief. He was going to hear me out. "That's right. I know this mountain like my own backyard. And Jonas was a friend of mine. We think Ski Northwest is out to sabotage-"

"Get out!" he yelled, and pointed at the door. I stared at him. "You and your little friends have been causing me enough problems. Who do you think you are coming in here and wasting my time with this ridiculous story?"

I kept trying. "Mr. Sorenson, I-I've done research and depth hoar isn't the problem. We've seen tracks out of bounds and besides snowboarders only the Ski Patrol goes out there. There's this new guy on the patrol with the fat powder skis and-"

"Now you're making unfounded accusations. Why am I listening to this?" He came out from behind his desk and strode towards me. "Get out of my office right now, kid, or you won't be allowed on this mountain again!" He crowded me back through the door and it slammed shut in my face.

CHAPTER 17

I excused myself after dinner and went to my room. I dialed Trevor's number and told him what we had to do.

"We better not get caught," he said. "My parents will ground me for life."

"We won't," I assured him. "Trust me. Just do as I tell you."

I got my things together: headlamp, dark clothes and gloves. I stuffed them into a knapsack.

"Mom," I called as I came out of my room. She and Brent were sitting close to one another on the couch in front of the fire. They looked, I don't know, kind of cozy sitting there. I decided I kind of liked having Brent around. "I'm just going over to Trevor's for a bit."

"OK, Tanner," she replied. She must have been distracted, since she didn't even ask me what time I'd be back. The dogs wanted to come outside with me but I shooed them back into the house. Not this time.

There was enough moonlight reflecting off the snow that I didn't need my headlamp. I walked down from our place into the valley. It was a cold crisp night and the old snow squeaked underfoot. I was glad there was no new snow. This way, our footprints would not be easy to see.

Trevor was waiting for me by the chain-link fence near the school. He, too, wore dark clothes and had a headlamp in his hand. I explained again what we had to do. He nodded and we headed towards the resort.

The only lights at the resort were from the grooming machines, high above us on the mountain slopes. These heavy tractors flatten out the frozen ridges of snow kicked up by the crowds of skiers during the day. The drivers work all night, and in the morning all the trails have a flat, slightly ridged surface like corduroy.

The Ski Patrol hut was dark. We stuck to the shadows anyway. The door was locked but there was a glass window in it. I hefted a rock experimentally.

"Are you sure you want to do this?" asked Trevor in a whisper.

"It's for the good of Sighing Pass," I whispered back. "We're on our own now and I need proof."

"Aren't they gonna wonder how the glass got broken?"

"I'll dump the rock later," I answered, "and we'll throw some snowballs against the side of the hut. It'll just look like kids were having a snowball fight and one broke the window. OK, ready?" We listened. There was no sound but the distant hum of the grooming machines.

Trevor nodded. It was the first willful act of vandalism I had ever committed and I hesitated a moment. Then I brought back my arm and let it fly. The sound of glass breaking was shockingly loud. We both froze, waiting to hear an alarm or the sound of someone coming, but there was nothing. My heart was pounding. I reached towards the hole in the glass and Trevor grabbed my arm.

"Wear your gloves!" he hissed.

I cursed at myself. *Slow down, you idiot! Think!*

The bulky snowboard glove knocked a few shards of glass off, which tinkled onto the floor inside. I reached around, unlocked the door, and opened it. I stepped inside, trying to avoid the glass on the floor as best I could, and I turned my headlamp on. It was pretty obvious why the hut only had a simple lock and no alarm system. There was nothing in the place except a desk and a couple of bare cots for hurt people to lie down on. I picked the rock up off the floor and scanned my headlamp around the walls. I could hear thudding noises as Trevor pounded snowballs against the side of the hut. Then, there it was, on the wall over the desk. The duty roster. I went over and squinted to make out the print. Saturday's date, the Saddle area, avalanche control ordered and the name of the patroller whose duty it had been.

"Tanner!" The whisper was urgent. "C'mon, someone's coming!"

I turned off my headlamp, hurried across the room, felt for the doorknob, turned the lock and pulled the door closed behind me. Trevor was crouched in the shadows. Together we scrambled up over a snow bank and lay on the other side, trying to breathe quietly. Nothing. We waited a few minutes longer. No one came. I dropped the rock I was still holding in my hand.

"Sorry, Tanner," Trevor finally broke the silence. "False alarm, I guess. I was getting a little freaked out. Did you get it?"

"Oh, yes," I said. "I sure did. And now we have a little trap to set for Mr. Jeff Arnott."

CHAPTER 18

The avalanche course was held at the school. It seemed strange to be walking down the halls and getting my binder out of my locker when it was dark outside. I saw that the class was pretty full. There were the other Surfers, along with a couple guys in their graduating year who we don't see out so often - and a whole lot of younger guys in grade nine and ten. I bet their parents were scared and made them come. There were also a group of girls and some guys I didn't recognize.

The instructor introduced himself as a Ski Patroller from a resort in the interior. He was also a fire fighter and the avalanche expert who was consulted when Calgary hosted the winter Olympics in 1988. He looked like one of those big burly types you see on real-life cop shows.

He started by telling us some grizzly stories about kids caught in avalanches, like how one kid's leg was broken in so many places when he wrapped around a tree that his thigh was curved in the shape of the letter C. And the kid who managed to dig himself out but couldn't find his friend and had to crawl to the road for help. They didn't find his friend for a month, because the poor guy was buried under four meters of snow and had a tree on top of him.

All the stuff you wish was true about avalanches isn't.

Like, can you out-ski or out-board one? Unlikely. Depending on whether the snow is wet or dry, avalanches can move at speeds from 20 to 200 km/h. Are you safe if you move across the base of a slope? Nope. You don't have to be on the slope to trigger an avalanche that will come down on top of you. Can you tunnel yourself out if you do get caught? Not a chance. Once soft snow gets churned and mixed around it sets hard like concrete, and within minutes, you're entombed. It's really hard to get out even if only your legs are buried. All pretty chilling stuff.

He made a good case for never going out of bounds, which makes a lot of sense if you aren't really interested in learning all this stuff. There are enough slopes within resort areas that are challenging enough for most people, and the halfpipe and the parks keep a lot of snowboarders out of trouble. There are other sports, though, the whole point of which is being out of bounds, like backcountry ski-touring, mountaineering, and climbing. For those folks, and for boarders like us who love being really out there, it's super-important to know what's going on with the snow.

There are about 12 deaths every year in Canada and 24 in the States from avalanches. Not a huge percentage of the people that hang out in the mountains. I guess if it happens to you, though, it's a hundred percent. Avalanches that kill people are usually triggered by people, so it's not a luck thing like getting struck by lightening.

The instructor gave us a break and we went to the cafeteria to get some pop. We were sitting around when a guy I hadn't seen before came up to us.

"Hey, are you Tanner?"

"Yeah." I was sure I didn't know him.

"Name's Mel. I e-mailed you a couple of weeks back."

"*Melvin?*" snickered Trevor. I slammed him with my elbow. He dug back at me with his.

"Nice win in Vermont," I said. Trevor stopped.

"Thanks."

"Are you, like, Mel Hawkins?" Trevor asked, looking embarrassed.

"Yeah."

Mel Hawkins was a bit of a superstar in snowboarding. He came from the Eastern Townships in Quebec and, at seventeen years old, took the halfpipe world by storm. This season he'd won two major eastern competitions.

"What are you doing *here*?" was all Trevor could manage. At least Mel seemed to have a sense of humor.

"Who's your friend?" he asked me. I introduced Trevor, and Xav, too.

"Sorry, dude," offered Trev. "Like, I had no idea..."

"Skip it," said Mel. "To answer your question, though, I came out for the contest at Quail and I've been hanging out with friends up here just freeriding. Our coach signed us all up for this course. We don't get too many avalanches in Quebec."

"Are you going to be around for the contest?" I asked.

Mel looked around before answering. "Our coach would kill us," he said, "but we're all into it. This contest is legend. Some of the guys have to go back East, but me and those two over there will be there. Do you need any help?"

The thought had crossed my mind. "Yeah, I just might. You'll need to pay attention to the course, though."

"A little bit of ditch-digging maybe, eh?"

"Maybe so."

"We can handle that."

After the break the course started to get more technical. I knew the first part. The cause of most avalanches starts with the snow. When we think of snow we usually think of the star-shaped flakes that we catch on our mittens as they fall. And everyone knows that no two flakes are exactly alike. But rarely do you see the pretty storybook crystals on the ground. New snow changes shape quickly. The spikes and feathered edges disappear and the crystals turn into round grains. When these grains stick together and have time to settle, the snowpack becomes very strong. But it isn't always so simple. The instructor did an OK job of dumbing down what was probably a pretty complicated scientific process.

"When the temperature of the snow down near the ground remains near freezing but the temperature of the snow on the surface is closer to the colder air temperature, heat rises up through the snowpack."

"Heat?" whispered Trevor. "It all seems pretty cold to me, dude."

The instructor overheard him. The guy was pretty good-natured. "It isn't really warm," he told Trevor, "all I'm saying is that there is enough difference between the temperature of the snow on the surface and the temperature six feet under for all this to happen."

He projected a diagram on the screen. "The heat melts a little bit of ice from each grain of snow and turns it into water vapor which is sucked up through the layers. The round grains of settled snow begin to change. Water melts from the tops of these grains and refreezes on the bottom of the grains above. It works like a chain reaction with each round grain shrinking at the top and growing on the bottom.

"The grains of snow don't look smooth anymore. Now

90

they're starting to look like diamonds cut into a pear shape, with corners and edges and flat faces. This process is called faceting; the snow develops "facets" just like the facets that a jeweler cuts into an expensive gem.

"The next stage is the one you've all heard about. Depth hoar. The grains have continued to lose ice at the top and gain it on the bottom until they look like little hollow cups. Cup-shaped crystals don't stick together very well. And they aren't as strong as the round solid grains because each crystal is just an empty air space surrounded by a thin sheath of ice. A layer of these crystals is very fragile. Under pressure, it will collapse.

"Now, we have to worry about this happening in Alberta a lot more than here near the coast. In the Rockies, where you'll find thinner snowpack and colder temperatures, depth hoar often develops next to the ground and near the surface of the snowpack. In these mountains, some slopes may remain unstable for an entire season."

"Can you imagine?" I asked Trev. "An entire season - that would be totally bogus."

"It's one reason why there isn't a lot of heli-skiing going on there," said the instructor. "But you folks have things quite a bit better." A few of the younger kids gave a half-hearted cheer and then stopped, embarrassed.

"In the mountains west of the Rockies, where you live, the snowpack is usually thick and the air milder. Thick snowpack and warmer temperatures result in the rounding of the snow crystals, so the snowpack is strengthened over a period of days or weeks. More likely in these mountains is for clear days and cold nights to cause a thin layer of facets to form on the surface. This weak layer can then become buried, but depth hoar is the exception rather than the rule."

I was thinking to myself that everything the instructor was saying just confirmed what I had learned on the Internet. It was possible that the occasional avalanche might be caused by depth hoar, but from what I had gathered, it was crazy to think that all the slides in Sighing Pass were the result of this snow-pack stuff. It wasn't the kind of problem that occurred just because we had unusual weather one winter.

Over the next few days we learned a lot. We'd meet outside after school and actually look at the snow and try practical tests and then later we'd have a lesson to set us up for the next day. It became obvious very quickly that determining snow safety wasn't the easiest thing in the world.

First you have to make observations that help you figure out how stable the snow probably is. You check out if there have been avalanches happening. You look for the effects of wind on the snow, like drifts, and cornices, and places where the wind has scoured away snow. You consider how much snow there is and what the weather has been like. Rain, lots of snow falling at once, or sudden changes in temperature affect snow stability. You check with the ranger station or the alpine club for reports. And then there are the tests.

I found out that we hadn't been digging our pits properly. We'd just been lucky so far not to have been caught in a slide, because our tests hadn't told us anything useful. Pits are dug to determine what layers lie beneath the surface of the snow. You need a straight, flat wall across the top of the pit and another at right angles going downhill. Of course you have to dig them with a shovel, and pretty deep too, two meters. Sometimes it's easy to see weak layers, sometimes not. You can draw a ruler or something down through the layers to check for resistance.

Another test involved cutting a column of snow from the edge of the pit with the shovel and then tapping it with the flat blade to see how much force it took for the column to compress as the weaker layers collapsed.

The most fun test of course, was the one everybody knows, the Rutschblock test. *Rutsch* means slide and that's what you do. You get on your skis or your board and stand on the hill just above the pit, and step, then jump, with more and more force - to see how much it takes for a slab of snow to break away from the side of the pit and dump you into the hole.

This is a lot of trouble to be sure that the slope you're going to ride will stay put, and then you have to take into consideration that tests usually make the slope seem ten percent more stable than they really are and even then you still only know about slopes that have the same pitch, elevation, and face the same way. It's a lot of work and it uses up a lot of time you'd rather spend riding, but I guess it's worth it.

The last thing that the instructor went over with us was what to do if you are caught in an avalanche. It would be a pretty wicked ride. All that snow mixed with trees and rocks. You have to try to get rid of your skis or board (easier said than done), and try to sort of swim to stay on the surface of the avalanche and work towards the side of the slide, grabbing at rocks or trees to try and slow yourself down. The last suggestion he had for us was the creepiest: Keep your mouth shut.

CHAPTER 19

"I guess the saddle's out of the question," said Trevor. We were sitting in the cafeteria at school talking about the contest. "It's too close to the resort anyway and now the snowpack will be totally bogus after that slide."

"Where are we going to hold it then?" I asked.

"Maybe we should find a new site," put in Xav. "Someplace new, farther away from the resort where there are no accidents this year."

"Any ideas, Tanner?" Trevor looked at me. I shrugged.

"I thought the saddle was the perfect place. It's where it was last year."

"Bucky and his friends organized it last year. Let's ask them. Maybe they know another good spot."

"I can get Jenny to find out. Those guys are all back in the city now."

"That's a good idea, Tanner," said Xav. "You find out a good spot and then the three of us will do a *reconnaissance*. It will be just like back in France when with my friends we would hear about a new place for snowboarding and then we would hike out in the mountains and find it."

I called Jenny as soon as I got home.

"Hi! How are you doing?" I asked.

"I'm doing great! What's up, Tanner?" She sounded really happy on the phone.

"Not much," I answered. "We're looking for a new site for the contest, though, and I need to ask you a favor."

"Ask away."

"Can you dial up Bucky on that computer of yours and see if he or any of his cronies know of a good spot? He was the man of this mountain after all and he would know."

"Sure, Tanner, I could do that, but..."

"But what?"

"Why don't you ask him yourself? He's right here!"

I heard her giggle and call to someone else. I suddenly felt numb and a bit nauseous. Bucky? What was he doing over at Jenny's? Was something going on between them? Since when? Could all this be happening to me? I nearly hung up and then I heard another voice on the other end of the line.

"Tanner!" It was Bucky's nasal drawl. "Hey, dude, it's been a while. Been hearin' all the news. Bogus tidings dude. Everybody's bummed about Jonas."

I tried to keep my voice steady and casual sounding. "Yeah, I know. You and the guys coming to the contest?"

"For sure. Wouldn't miss it, dude. What's happening with you guys anyway? Need any help?"

"Yeah, we could use some judges."

"No problem, anything else?"

"We were gonna hold it over past the saddle, but the slope was manky and it slid."

"Yeah, I heard. Spooky. That's usually a solid spot, dude."

"I know. So we need to find someplace else. You got any ideas?" There was a pause. My face was burning and I fought the desire to slam the phone down. How could he move in on my girlfriend like that and talk to me on the phone like nothing was up?

"East, dude."

"What?"

"East, further down the valley. It's a bit of a hike but there's some sweet terrain over there. Take the farthest chair to the top, head down the trail until you clear out of sight and then start climbing up the ridge towards the Sentinel. There're some good gaps and a big bowl over there, and most of it's below the tree line so it won't be so obvious. We used to head over there whenever they were really nailing us for going OB."

I tried to think of where he meant. The east side had mostly easy intermediate trails, so we didn't go there much. I didn't think there was anything past the last trail; the Sentinel was the next peak over and had no ski resort development on it. "OK, we'll check it out."

"Yeah, and keep it quiet, dude."

"Tanner?" It was Jenny's voice on the line again.

"Yeah?" I tried to sound as cool as I could.

"I'll be coming up for the contest with Bucky and the guys in their van. Word's been getting around at Quail and in the interior. I think we'll get a good turnout."

"Good." I said. "See ya, then."

"OK, see ya. Oh yeah, Tanner?"

"Yeah?" I hoped she'd say something about us, that she missed me, was looking forward to seeing me, anything.

"Bucky and I'll post the new location on the Net, OK?"

"Cool," I said. "That'd be great."

"OK. Call me." And she hung up.

On Friday night the Surfers got together to plan our

reconnaissance trip for the next day. Trevor and Xav were over at my house and we were down in the basement sorting gear.

"Do we really need all this stuff?" asked Trevor. "I mean, if it's only like an hour of bushwhacking each way, then why do we need to take sleeping bags and a stove?" I myself was in favor of going as light as possible, and to be honest my heart wasn't really in this mission. I was totally preoccupied with imagining Jenny and Bucky together and feeling lousy about it. But Xav was insistent.

"*C'est les montagnes*," he said. "You must always be prepared. Anything can happen there, even if it is only a short hike. Tomorrow we must prepare for every part of our plan. We will be out a long time and no one will know where we are going, so if we have trouble, we have to help ourselves." I looked at the pile of gear on the floor. We had sleeping bags, a tarp in case we needed a shelter, headlamps, a stove, some dehydrated soup and some chocolate, a map and two compasses and a shovel each that collapsed, telescope fashion, to fit on the outside of our packs.

"Where did you get all this stuff?" asked Trevor.

"From my father," replied Xav. "He doesn't mind if I borrow it and he doesn't ask too many questions. He thinks it's good that I go make my own adventures in the mountains. It's the way that he learned. And don't wear the clothes like it is an afternoon at the halfpipe, eh?" he continued. "No cotton, only synthetic and many layers, and extra mittens, OK?"

Trev and I nodded. We both thought mountaineering was really cool, but we haven't done anything more than some winter hiking and camping, so we listened to Xav when it came to more serious stuff. He'd been doing this kind of thing for years with his dad and he knew what he was talking about. We divvied up all the gear and started stuffing it in our packs.

"How are we going to get past the lifties with all this stuff?"
I asked. "It looks like we're planning to stay out a week!"

Xav looked over at me. "This operation, *c'est clandestin..*
We're not taking the lift."

"Then how are we getting up there?"

He smiled. "By our feet."

"No way!" interrupted Trevor. "It will take us half the day
just to hike up the valley as far as the Sentinel and everyone in
town will see us."

Xav grinned. "Alpine start," he said. "I'll see you at 4:00.
And that's 4:00 in the morning, Trevor. So you better go to bed
right now. But don't worry too much, I have a special sur-
prise."

I told my mom that I was planning to leave early that day,
but she had no idea how early. Even the dogs didn't bother to
get out of bed to see what I was up to. I let myself quietly out
of the house at 3:30 and shouldered my pack in the driveway.
It was pretty dark so I turned on my headlamp and started
down the road. I couldn't see the moon or any stars.

It took me about 25 minutes to get to Xav's house. The
walk had warmed me up and I had taken off my outer shell and
put it in my pack. Getting overheated in winter is almost as
dangerous as getting too cold. When you're hot, you sweat.
That moisture stays in your clothes and when you slow down
or stop, it freezes. Then you're cold and clammy, and you
won't warm up again until you start moving or change clothes.
We were always adding and removing layers of clothing to stay
comfortable. I learned long ago not to breathe into my mitts
to warm up my hands, either. The moisture from my breath
froze and I got a painful case of frostnip. I might as well have

stuffed wet snow into them for all the good it did me.

The guys were waiting for me beside a bulky, lumpy object covered by a tarp. As I came closer, Xav awkwardly yanked back the stiffly frozen tarp. *"Voila!"* he cried.

"Wicked!" breathed Trevor. "Snowmobiles!" Two well-used snowmobiles stood ready to go. "Are we allowed?"

"Oh yes," said Xav. "My father lends them to us. Come on, let's go."

We strapped two packs on the back of Xav's snowmobile. I wore the third and got on the other machine behind Trevor. We started the engines and headed east along the ravine that skirts the edge of town and continued up the valley. There were very few lights on in any of the houses we passed by. I could occasionally see the flashing strobes of the grooming machines high above us on the mountain.

Soon we were on the snow-covered fire road and heading well away from town. This road wasn't used much in the winter and was never ploughed. The far end of it marked the trailhead for summer hiking trails up to Sentinel Mountain. We cruised up the road on the snowmobiles. The snow was deep and we weren't following any tracks. As I hung on to Trevor and tried to shelter myself from the cold wind, I thought about Jenny some more.

We arrived at the east side of Sighing Mountain by about 5:00 a.m. It was still dark. I couldn't see the silhouettes of either Sighing Mountain to the west or Sentinel to the east. We gathered in front of Xav's snowmobile and held the map in the headlights to look at it.

"I made a route on the map," explained Xav. "You see this line here. It goes up the side of the steep gully in front of us and then from the top of the gully we go on this bearing, south east, towards Sentinel. That will take us to the bowl Bucky was talking about. Do you want to navigate, Tanner?"

"Yeah, sure," I answered and took the big mountaineering compass from him. We strapped on our snowshoes and shouldered our packs. I took a bearing up the gully from where the snowmobiles were. I lined the direction of travel arrow up the gully, now visible in the gray dawn light and turned the compass housing until the magnetic arrow lined up with the arrow painted on the bottom of the compass. There was another, adjustable arrow as well as the one painted on. I didn't know what it was for so I lined it up with the housing too. "170°" I read from the index line. "Let's go."

We started up the steep slope. It was tricky maneuvering the snowshoes around small trees sticking out from the snow, but I was glad to have them. Without them we would have sunk up to our hips.

It was hard work. Stamp the snowshoe into the snow, step up on it. Stamp in the other one, step up. I had to climb bowlegged to avoid stepping on my own feet and soon I felt hot from the effort and took my hat off. After a while I found a rhythm in the climbing and my thoughts drifted to Jenny again. I wanted to ask her what was going on, but I didn't want to seem jealous. I resolved not to call her until she called me. We continued up the gully. After about an hour I called a short rest. We stood there breathing hard.

"How're you guys doing?"

"All right," answered Trevor. "Are we nearly at the top?"

"We're almost there!" called out Xav, pointing up. I could see the gully join a ridge line a hundred meters or so further. We continued floundering up through the snow.

About ten minutes later we reached some level ground. It

was a relief to stand upright and not be leaning into a slope anymore. Trees grew thickly all around and we couldn't see either Sighing or Sentinel Mountain anymore. It was full daylight, finally, but overcast and gray. It had started to snow lightly. From where we stood it was a moderate treed slope without any other visible landmarks.

I pulled out the big compass and turned the housing so that a bearing of 135° or southeast, showed at the index line. Then I turned my body so that the magnetic needle lined up with the painted arrow. The direction of the travel arrow indicated where we should go. I pointed up the slope and squinted to find a landmark. "That way! Straight to that dark tree next to the cedar!"

"There're too many trees for snowshoes!" called out Trevor.

"He's right!" agreed Xav. "I'm carrying mine!" I tried a few steps but after nearly tripping twice, I had to agree. I took a few minutes to strap them to my pack and then continued on, sinking in up to my knees. Once we got to the tree I had identified I sighted another landmark, a broken branch, along the same bearing. We climbed to that one, then looked for something else to head towards. The trees were thick enough that we had to duck around trunks and under branches. It was hard work and it seemed to go on forever.

"There's something dark up there!" called out Trevor. "What is it?"

"I don't know!" I yelled back. "We should be topping out at the edge of the bowl soon, though!"

"That is not a bowl," said Xav tersely from right behind me. "That's a cliff. Where the heck are we?"

He was right. A few moments later we came to a dead

end. We were at the bottom of a sheer cliff and it was about fifty meters high!

CHAPTER 20

"Tanner! What has happened?" Xav was asking me. I was standing on a boulder staring up at the cliff.

"I don't know," I answered him. "I thought I was following the bearing OK."

"Let me see the compass," he said. I passed it over to him. I heard him swear softly.

"What is it?" I asked.

"You forgot the declination," he said. "We are off route. That's why I gave you my father's compass, so you would not need to do the math."

"What do you mean?" I asked.

"This compass has an arrow here, the extra one." He indicated the arrow I hadn't known what to do with. "You need to adjust it to 12° east of magnetic north and use it to line the magnetic needle up, instead of the arrow painted on the compass. That is how you get the true bearing."

I cursed myself. The declination. It was the same mistake I'd made in geography class. How could I have done it again? And out here! Where it really mattered.

"Are we lost?" I asked him.

"Not yet," he answered, pulling out the map. "I think we can still figure out where we are." We all bent over the waterproof map case. Xav put the compass on it and lined it up with the top of the gully using the bearing I had followed. "That would have taken us," he followed the line of travel with his finger, "here! We're at the bottom of this cliff face here. We're too far west now and this is a cliff band on the side of Sentinel." It was obvious once he'd pointed it out. My mistake had taken us almost a kilometer off course.

"What do we do now?" asked Trevor.

"First we have something to eat and drink," answered Xav, "and then we follow the bottom of this cliff east for about a kilometer and we will find the bowl. It's OK. We're not lost after all."

Xav was right. After a rest and some hot soup we felt much happier. It was pretty rough going across the boulders at the base of the cliff but at least we knew where we were and we made good time. Even so, it was almost noon by the time we reached the ridge of the bowl we'd been aiming for.

Bucky knew the mountain all right. This bowl would be perfect for our needs. The slope was steep at the top and then leveled out a bit. It was long enough, there were a few rock outcrops you could jump off if you wanted and plenty of space for a kicker at the bottom. It was low enough that there were a few trees poking up above the snow. That would reduce the chance of avalanche. We looked around for signs of a recent slide. There were no fracture lines where slabs of snow had broken away. I couldn't see any broken trees. The one negative thing was that it was a bit of a terrain trap, since there wasn't a clear escape route out of the whole bowl.

I was relieved to see there were no tracks of any kind. And best of all, there were lots of places in the rocks along the ridge for people to hang out, hide and, well, keep an eye on things, just like in my plan. Trevor and Xavier pulled their shovels out of their packs and started digging a pit. I attached some colored flagging tape to a few rocks to mark the places I had in mind.

"Wish I had my board with me," said Trevor, leaning on his shovel and looking wistfully at the slope. "First tracks would be awesome in there"

"Relax, Trev," I said. "What we're doing is way more important."

"I know, I know. But I just want to ride, dude."

"You will, you'll see. It's more important to save this resort than it is than to enter one little contest. Trust me."

"Trust you, declination man?"

I had to laugh. "OK. Don't trust me. Just do as I say."

It took a while to finish the pit. We dug it extra deep, just to be sure. We tried all the tests we'd learned in the course. Not once did the snow we tested fail at any level. The Rutschblock test was pretty fun. Trevor and Xavier both got on their snowshoes and jumped up and down above the pit like a couple of idiots. It didn't slide in a block, but kind of caved in slowly after a while.

"I think it's pretty good," said Xav. "But perhaps we should dig another." So we headed down the bowl to where it became less steep. It was harder to dig the pit here because you had to pitch the snow higher to clear the hole out. I had to take off my jacket, I got so hot from the exertion. The results were pretty much the same, although we didn't dig the pit quite as deep. Afterwards we slogged up the bowl to the ridge again.

Xav spoke up. "We better get going. The snow is falling more now." I looked around. It was snowing pretty hard, and with no tall trees on the ridge where we were it was getting hard to tell the white ground from the white fog that surrounded us. The wind was making the weird whistling noise that Sighing Pass was named for. With this extra snow, we would have to retest the slope on the day of the contest. I gave myself a mental reminder to e-mail Mel when I got home.

"Take another bearing, declination man, and let's get out of here," said Trevor. This time I knew what I was doing. I set a bearing for northwest, the opposite direction to the one we should have come here by, and lined up the magnetic needle with the declination arrow. The direction of travel pointed down into the trees, which all looked the same through the heavy snow.

"This is going to be hard if we can't pick landmarks to head for," I said. "Trev, do you have the other compass?"

"Sure," he said, digging it out. "You want me to navigate too?"

"Kind of," I replied. "You'll be the moving landmark. Follow a bearing of northwest until we can still just see you. We'll yell to keep you on the bearing and to tell you when to stop. Then you can double check we're on course by taking a bearing back to us. It should be exactly southeast. Then you just stand there and-"

"And then you two will catch up with me," he continued. "And then I'll go out in front again. That way you'll have a landmark to follow, and I'll be double-checking the bearing each time."

"Very good idea!" called Xav from below us on the slope. "But lets get going. The storm is getting worse and I'm getting cold!"

Our plan worked like a charm. Trevor, who had too much

energy anyway, would bound down in front until we could just barely see him through the snow. Then we'd yell for him to stop and then get him to stand in line with our bearing. He'd yell back that he'd checked the bearing back to us and then Xav and I would catch up. And then we'd repeat the whole process. Xav wasn't doing so well, though. He was complaining about the cold more and more and starting to stumble a bit. I was a little worried about him. People think it's much easier to go downhill than up, but that's not always the case. On a steep hill you have to use your leg muscles to slow yourself down, and it gets really tiring. Snowshoes are useless on the way down and in our boots we sunk deep in the snow with every step. Twice, Xav slipped and sat down suddenly, and the second time he wanted to stay and rest. It took a lot of convincing to get him up and moving again.

I heard a whoop from Trevor ahead of us. The gully! Our bearing had led us directly back to the top of it. We caught up with him a few minutes later. He slapped me on the back. "Way to go, declination man! Your plan worked!" We weren't out of the woods yet, though

"Trev, I think we have to stop and rest," I said. "Xav's freezing."

"I don't feel good," mumbled Xav, flopping down in the snow. "My stomach hurts."

Trevor looked at him. "Maybe we should just keep going," he said. "It's only another hour to the trailhead, maybe less."

"No," I disagreed with him. "He'd better warm up now or he might not make it down." Trevor reluctantly agreed, and we dug into our packs. I made Xav sit on an empty pack and wrapped him in a sleeping bag. Trevor poured a little bit of water from his Thermos into a pot and filled the rest up with snow. That was something Xav had shown us before. You can't just melt snow in a dry pot without it taking forever and tasting really funny. Then Trevor fired up the stove and started heating it for soup. Even so, it took a long time to get the water hot. We stretched the tarp over our heads. There wasn't much wind down amongst the trees, but the snow was still coming down heavily and made a pattering sound on the tarp. Eventually the water was ready and Trevor poured in the soup mix, stirred it up and passed it around. Xav didn't want any but I forced him to have some. Pretty soon he perked up and started talking a bit.

"I didn't know how thirsty I was," he said. "I should have known to stop earlier. But I think I'm OK, now. We should get going." We packed up as quickly as possible and started down the gully. We half walked, half slid most of the way down, and pretty much tobogganed the last 50 meters to the snowmobiles on our butts. The machines were now completely covered with snow. They looked like moguls. I checked my watch. It was nearly five o'clock and starting to get dark.

We brushed off the two machines and started back down the fire road. Our tracks from the morning had disappeared. It was hard to see through the blowing snow, but somehow the trip back up the fire road seemed shorter than on the way in. We returned the snowmobiles to the heliport and then we stood and joked around for a bit, pleased with ourselves for finding our way back down to the gully in the storm. Xavier seemed to have found some extra energy somewhere and tried to wash my face with snow. I checked him into a snow bank.

"If we can do that, we can do anything, man!" said Trevor.

"You guys did a good job," said Xav. "I think your plan for

the contest will work, Tanner. Maybe there is 10 or 15 centimeters of new snow, but there is time before the contest for it to settle."

"If it doesn't," I replied, "we'll have to cancel it or do something else. Anyway, it's getting late and I'm starved. If it gets too much later, folks will be out looking for us. We'd better head on home."

CHAPTER 21

I was pretty tired when I got home, but not too tired to be thinking about Jenny. Or Jenny and Bucky, to be exact. OK, so he was a couple of years older, but so what? I considered myself to be pretty cool for sixteen. I looked at myself in the mirror: average height, short brown hair, didn't need braces. Not bad. Bucky certainly wasn't a better rider than I was, not anymore, anyway. I used to look up to him when I was younger and first venturing onto the halfpipe. I used to be so self-conscious. I was so nervous of wiping out that I wouldn't even let myself ride up to the top of the pipe. I would crank a turn lower down, where I felt safer. The pipe would get pretty icy and I'd stop even trying. I'd hang out in the park near a jump or something, instead.

One day, though, things just changed. It was after I started hanging around with Trevor and Jonas. They weren't all that good either, but they wanted to be. Neither of them cared if they ended up sliding down most of the pipe on their butts. It didn't hurt. And we were all lousy at it. Pretty soon, I didn't care what anyone else thought either. In fact, if we fell, we would mock each other far worse than the older guys would. And then when the older guys said something, it felt like nothing. That's what was so good about hanging out with the

Surfers. Out of the three of us, or the four once Xav came to town, someone would have whatever it took.

I picked up the phone and called Trevor. Maybe he would know what I should do about Jenny.

"Yeah?" he sounded like he was half asleep.

"Hey, Trev, it's me, Tanner."

"Tanner, what's the matter with you, dude? Didn't you get enough exercise today? What are you still doing up? Heading off to aerobics or something? Dance class?"

"Shut up. What do you think about Bucky?"

"Bucky? He's cool, why?"

"No, I mean do you think he'd move in on your girlfriend if you weren't around?"

"My girlfriend? What girlfriend? He could move in all he wants 'cause there's nobody there."

"No, that's not what I mean." I told him about my phone call to Jenny's house.

"Oh. I don't know, Tanner, that girl seems too nice. I don't think she'd do that. But with Bucky I guess you just don't know."

"How come this sort of thing never happened to Jonas? He had the girls wrapped around his finger. They put up with all kinds of crazy stuff from him. And the stuff at school after he died. It's like he was Jim Morrison, or a movie star or something. Like that guy in the movie Titanic who dies. Girls go to a cemetery in Halifax and leave flowers on the grave of some poor dude with the same name who wasn't anything like the character in the movie."

Trevor was quiet for a while. Then he gave me a pretty serious answer.

"I saw that movie. I saw it with a girl, too. You know what,

Jonas was a little bit like a character in a movie, Tanner. Not that he was some kind of hero or anything, but he was really nice to girls. They love that. He may have talked the way he did with us, you know, all cool and everything, but I heard him on the phone with them. He'd call them back and stuff, and he didn't try to play head games with them. Even his ex-girl-friends didn't hate him. Remember Jane at the memorial ser-vice?"

I did. She'd been dumped by Jonas after more than a year of seeing him and she had been so upset she'd had to leave the gym.

"You should just call Jenny and ask her what's up, Tanner. Or go see her. That's what Jonas would have done. And besides, you're not doing a very good job of playing it cool, dude. Gotta go, I'm bagged." And he hung up.

I found myself on a bus to the city the next Friday. I got a call from the rehab clinic and was told that my knee brace was ready. They wanted me to come in to try it out and to make sure it was adjusted properly.

The bus was pretty empty, so I stowed my stuff in the overhead bin and grabbed a window seat. I watched the scenery go by and thought of Jenny. It had been a week since our last conversation, and despite what Trevor had said, I still hadn't called her. Then again, she hadn't called me, either. I was surprised how crappy I felt about the whole thing. I could-n't get her out of my mind. I kept asking myself questions. Would she really do that? Would she just can me and start see-ing Bucky and not even have the guts to tell me? Even if we had only been seeing each other for a couple of weeks, we'd been through a lot. I felt like she was my girlfriend now, not just some girl I'd met at a party who I talked to on the phone.

I just couldn't imagine her doing something so brutal. It didn't seem like her. It didn't make sense.

As we came down out of the mountains there was less snow. Dead grass and brush poked up to form patterns of rust brown on white. The road was gray-black with slush.

I hate city bus terminals. They all have the same feeling about them whether they're in Vancouver, Toronto, or San Francisco. It's kind of like a cloud of disappointment, as if people arrive in the city with big hopes and dreams and then end up having to go back to where they came from, with all their money spent and everything they own in old duffel bags shoved into the stainless steel storage compartments on the bus' underbelly. In the movies, bus terminals also seem like human hunting grounds, for low-lifes, pimps and pickpockets. Not that I'd know one to see one, or ever had anything ripped-off, but I always hung on to my stuff just in case and didn't hang around.

My dad said he'd try to pick me up, but if he didn't show to head on over to his place. There wasn't any sign of him so I took a cab over to the condo. My dad wasn't there either. When I listened to the messages on the answering machine there was one from him saying he'd be home late. There was also a message from Jenny. I was so relieved to hear her voice I played it twice.

"Hey Tanner, I called your mom's and she said you were heading into town so I thought I'd try you at your dad's place. Haven't heard from you for a while and I've got lots to tell you so give me a call when you get in. Bye." She sounded pretty normal. I was getting really confused. I checked my watch. 9:00. Not too late to call if I wanted to. I went to the fridge and helped myself to a Coke. What was it that she had to tell me? Was it about Bucky? I thought about calling her back but I couldn't think of how to start a conversation with her, so I didn't.

I wandered around the condo for a while. I saw that my dad had bought himself a new digital video disc player, one of those new VCR things that use a CD instead of a VHS cassette. Must have cost him a bundle. Dad had never owned a VCR because he hated the technology behind it. He said it reminded him of the 8-track tape deck, some short-lived audio format from way before my time. I opened a hard case lying next to it. Inside was a DVD camcorder to go with it. Wow. I wondered what he was planning to do with it. He was the kind of guy who never had film in the camera when it came time for birthdays or Christmas.

I picked up the camcorder and turned it over it my hands. It was tiny. I could wrap one hand around it easily. There was a disc inside it. I hit play and looked through the lens. A figure started moving across a room. I recognized my dad's dining room. It was a woman, a pretty woman, in a black dress. She was lighting candles on the table. She looked up and laughed, then picked up a wine glass and toasted the camera. I pressed stop and put the camera down. I felt totally weird, kind of guilty and embarrassed, like I had been caught spying on someone. I put the camera back into the case and snapped it shut. Just then I heard keys in the door, and voices in the hall.

"Tanner?" It was my dad and he had someone with him. "Are you there?"

"Yeah!" I called back. "Hi Dad." I walked over to the entrance hall. My dad was hanging up a woman's coat. He was talking to her. They both turned and smiled at me.

"Tanner, I'd like you to meet someone. This is Karen."

"Hi, Tanner." She was the same woman from the video.

"Hi," I said.

"I've been waiting for you to come to the city before telling you about Karen," my dad continued. "I've been looking forward to introducing the two of you. Karen and I are, well, we're sort of seeing each other."

I'd gathered that much. I nodded.

"Do you drink coffee?" She was asking me.

I nodded. "Sometimes."

"Good, I'll go make some." She headed for the kitchen. Certainly seems to know her way around, I thought.

"How long are you staying?" my dad asked.

"For the weekend, I guess. I pick up my knee brace tomorrow morning."

"Your friend Jenny's been calling."

"Yeah, I know. I got her message." We joined Karen in the kitchen. The coffee was almost ready and she had cups out and cookies and everything. She seemed nice and all, but I was still pretty shocked at having her there. She was trying to make friendly conversation with me and I didn't have the heart to be rude to her.

"I hear you do a lot of snowboarding up at Sighing Pass."

"Yeah." I twisted a paper napkin around my finger.

"I hadn't heard much about that name until recently, but now I'm running across it a lot at work."

She had my full attention now. "Why's that?" I asked.

"I work for the insurance company that insures Sighing Pass Resort."

"No kidding." I tried to think as fast as I could. "I guess there have been a lot of claims lately, huh?"

She poured me a cup of coffee. "That's an understatement. I don't think any insurance company can afford to continue providing coverage for that place."

"What will your company do about it?"

"We're planning to send someone up to inspect the place next week." She shrugged. "If the resort is judged to be unsafe then maybe we'll have to raise their premiums, or restrict how much insurance coverage they can have."

"What if they can't afford the cost of insurance?" I asked.

"They might have to close down. Legally, they can't operate unless they're fully insured." She gave me a closer look. "How come you're so interested in all this?"

"Yeah, Tanner," my dad said. "I thought you hated talking about the business world."

Maybe I'd pushed too hard. I shrugged. "I'd just be totally bummed out if it closed." They both seemed content with my response. I finished my coffee and excused myself.

CHAPTER 22

I told my dad and Karen that I was going for a walk. My dad spoke to me outside in the hall as I was waiting for the elevator.

"I didn't mean to keep anything a secret." he was saying.

"What?" I wasn't following what he meant.

"I mean Karen and me. It's not that I didn't want you to know about her."

"It's OK, Dad, really." He must have thought I was upset about his new girlfriend. "I just want to get some fresh air."

It was cold and wet outside and there were hardly any people on the street. I started walking fast. I was running this new information through my head. The insurance inspection couldn't be happening at a better time. If only there were some way to show them what was really happening at the resort. But how? Invite the inspector to the contest? I didn't think so. My last meeting with Resort Management hadn't been the most encouraging. I hated being a teenager sometimes. People just didn't take you seriously enough. I needed to talk to Jenny. She would have some ideas on how to pull it all together.

I turned on to Woodview. I was only a few blocks away from Brighton and Molten Java. I wondered if Jenny was working. I approached the coffee shop. It was still open so I went inside.

She was there. She had her coat on and she was talking to another waitress behind the counter. She turned around towards the door and our eyes met. I smiled at her. She walked towards me.

"Hey," I said softly. She brushed by me, pushed the door open and went outside. I followed her. "Hey!" I said louder. "Jenny?"

"What do you want?" She was still walking. I had to jog to catch up to her.

"I want to talk to you."

"Why now?"

"What do you mean?" I asked her. "C'mon, Jenny, slow down." She just started walking faster. "C'mon," I said again and reached for her hand. "Talk to me, Betty?" She jerked her hand away and turned around to face me. I was surprised to see tears streaking her cheeks.

"Why haven't you returned any of my calls?" she asked, wiping her eyes impatiently with her mitt. "Why are you here now when I haven't heard from you in over a week? Why should I talk to you now?"

"I'm sorry, I couldn't call you."

"Why not?"

"I didn't know what to say, how to ask you."

"Ask me what?"

"About Bucky."

"What about Bucky?"

"If you were seeing him or not. When I called you and he was there..."

"What are you talking about?" Her eyes looked huge

under the streetlights. "How could you even think that? He just stopped over for a little while because I asked him to. I was doing it for you. I was trying to get him to help you with the contest. What did you think I was doing?"

I suddenly felt pretty stupid. I didn't know what to say.

"I can't believe you didn't trust me," she said. "And I missed you, Tanner. It really hurt when you didn't call or answer my e-mails."

"I'm so sorry, Jenny," I said. I put my arms around her. She didn't move or try to push me away. I hugged her hard. I felt her head rest against my shoulder. "You're so amazing, and I am so sorry," I said.

She didn't want the people at the coffee shop to see her looking upset so we just walked around the streets for a while and talked. I was so relieved to find out that she wasn't seeing Bucky. I should have had a little more faith in her. She had been working really hard at promoting the contest to the snowboarders at Quail. There were probably going to be about forty of them coming. She'd even found most of them a place to stay at the Sighing Pass youth hostel, and the others all knew someone with a floor they could crash on. Bucky and a couple of his friends, older guys, would come to judge the contest and they would even build the kicker for us.

Her little mittened hand felt really good in mine as we walked along. Every couple of blocks I couldn't help pulling her into a store doorway and kissing her. I finally told her what I had wanted to tell her that last time I'd phoned, about me and Trevor breaking into the Ski Patrol hut and finding out who was in charge of controlling the slope by the Saddle the day we'd gone heli-boarding.

"It certainly does all add up," she said. "I can't believe

they wouldn't listen to you. Just because you're a teenager and a snowboarder no one takes you seriously. It makes me so mad."

I told her about the trap I was planning to set.

"All we can prove, though," I continued "is that someone is out to hurt snowboarders. I can't really prove that Ski Northwest is behind all of this even though I know everything is connected: the other avalanches, our boards getting vandalized, the grooming machine driver getting buried alive, even Jonas' accident. It's too bad we couldn't convince the insurance company that Sighing Pass is being sabotaged."

"What insurance company?" Jenny asked. I told her about my dad's new girlfriend and what she had said about the insurance inspection.

"Yeah, well, maybe you should put it to Trevor and Xav," she suggested. "You're not the only one who has good ideas, you know. I think you underestimate your friends. They might be able to help."

I winced. "I am really sorry, Jenny." She smiled.

"Like, for example, you have no idea of what high tech wonders I might be able to arrange for your little plan."

"What do you mean?" I was confused.

"Do you remember I told you I was working on an independent project for my geography teacher?"

"Yeah."

"Well, there's some equipment in the geography department that I think might come in useful."

"Like what?"

"Well, you remember the avalanche beacons we used when we went heli-boarding?"

"Really?' I asked. "He'd let you borrow avalanche beacons from the geography department? That's great! We could really use those."

"These are the latest technology. They work like two way radios, too."

"Wow."

"And that's not all." She grinned. "These also have G.P.S. locator systems built right in. We can radio our exact positions to each other."

I was astounded. I'd heard of these new beacons. They were equipped with a Global Positioning Satellite capability that meant the position of the beacon could be pinpointed to one square meter of accuracy by a signal sent to, and reflected from, a satellite. We would have no need for compasses or declination arrows.

"That's the coolest thing I've ever heard of. They must be worth a thousand bucks apiece. Are you sure he'll let you take them?"

She nodded. "I told him I'm planning to enter my Independent Study in the city science competition and I need-ed to finish some field research. He told me I'm welcome to borrow any of the equipment in the lab. And that would include the communications equipment. Take them, Tanner. There's no room for error on that day. There's a lot at stake."

"Jenny. I don't know what to say."

"Say thank you."

"Thank you." I picked her up and swung her around.

"Oh, and one more thing," she said, smiling. "I'm coming to the contest. And, I get to be in on the plan or I'm going home and I'm taking all my toys with me."

She kind of had me there.

I ended up staying at my dad's for the whole weekend. I

went to the rehab center on Saturday to pick up my knee brace. The physiotherapist who'd been helping me out was there, and she asked me put on some shorts and do a couple of exercises for her.

"Not bad, not bad," she said as I demonstrated that I had pretty much full range of motion when I bent and straightened my knee. "Can you show me a couple of squats?" I stood on the injured leg, squatted low and stood up. She nodded. "You've really come along well, and you've been icing it regularly, haven't you?"

"Yeah."

"And you've been snowboarding regularly too, haven't you?"

I laughed. "Yeah."

She crouched down to take a better look. "I can't see any swelling in comparison with the other one." She pulled out a tape measure and measured around each of my quads, then my calves. She stood up. "Not only have you managed to put back on the muscle that you lost," she said, "but the thigh and the calf of your injured leg are actually larger than on your normal side. You kids recover so quickly. I wish my other patients were so lucky. Now, I think you'd better either start exercising the other side as well, or the difference between the two is going to throw off your gait."

"Gait?"

"The way you walk," she explained. "For you, though, since you're so active anyway, I'd just stick to your normal activity. The two legs will even out. Wear your brace for field sports or court sports or if you're snowboarding in heavy wet snow. Otherwise, I think you're fine."

"Great. Thanks."

"That's wonderful!" was Jenny's response when I told her. "Now I don't have to go so easy on you when we go boarding." It was Saturday night and we were at a bowling alley, of all places, with a couple of her friends. Not that anyone bowls seriously of course, but when you're sixteen, there aren't a lot of places, other than movies, where you can hang out. Her friends were pretty funny in their stupid two-tone rental shoes and nearly every ball went into the gutter. Jenny got one strike and did a little dance on the polished wooden floor. She looked great.

The place was crowded with regulars who seemed to resent the intrusion. We didn't really fit in with the others in their close-fitting Levis and leather baseball jackets - which of course made us want to draw even more attention to ourselves. It was smoky, and there was a lot of noise from the bowling lanes and the arcade at the back of the place.

"So the reconnaissance went OK?" asked Jenny as she sat beside me on the little bench. We watched our scores show up on a ceiling-mounted television screen. I was losing.

"Well, yeah."

"Is the slope safe?" She shuddered. "I'll never forget that day in the helicopter. I don't think it's possible to be any more scared than that."

"You did fine," I told her. "I was the one that was too slow to react. I think the bowl's fine. We did all the tests and the snowpack seems good. I've arranged with Mel and his team mates for them to do another test the morning of the contest. We won't take any chances on the kids who're coming."

"It's so cool that you've gotten to know Mel Hawkins. All my friends are in love with him."

"He's an all right guy. He may have the sponsorships and

all that stuff, but he's still into snowboarding for the fun of it, you know? He's even found a bunch of routes that riders can use to get to the site, so not everyone is seen heading off down the same trail. And it was his idea to build a kicker for the little guys to use, right at the east edge of the resort."

"What for?"

"It's just to throw the casual observer off. Everyone will think boarders are heading over to watch this little contest when actually-"

"When actually the real contest is taking place over in the next bowl. That's a good idea. So pretty much everything is set, isn't it? We have the place, all the gear, lots of riders are coming from the city..."

"It's not the riders I'm worried about."

"Oh, come on, Tanner, what else can you do? From the perspective of anyone who dislikes snowboarders, this is exactly the sort of thing they hate. Snowboarders out of bounds, flouting the rules and making the management look silly."

"I wish there was just some way that we could get the people that matter to see what's really happening. Like the insurance adjuster my dad's girlfriend told me about. Not that anyone would listen. I tried that route."

"Jenny!" One of her friends was calling her.

"Give it a rest, Tanner," she said, and stood up to retrieve a burgundy bowling ball from the ball return chute. "C'mon, we're *bowling*!"

I gave her a smile, but I was thinking, *How can I make them all see?*

When I left Sunday night for Sighing Pass I was carrying some extra luggage: my dad's brand new DVD video camera.

CHAPTER 23

There was one point during the week when I thought that somehow we'd blown the whole thing. I was sitting in home-room trying to finish up some math that was due in the next period, when the principal came in to our homeroom class. He had a message for us.

"I'm coming around to each class individually," he said, "because I want you all to listen carefully. There's been some vandalism at the ski resort. Now, no one is accusing students at Sighing Pass of anything, but the area manager, Mr. Sorenson, has asked for our co-operation and I have decided to take this very seriously."

A guy in my class put his hand up. "What did they do?"

"Sorry, who?"

"The vandals. What did they do?"

"There were some windows broken, some items stolen, and some graffiti was spray painted on the side of one of the equipment sheds."

A girl at the back of the class piped up. "What'd it say?"

The class laughed.

The principal gave a little smile. "Not what you think. Initials of some sort or other. And there were windows broken at the Ski Patrol hut and in Mr. Sorenson's office." I felt a sudden chill. The principal was still speaking. "Again, no one is accusing anyone here of these crimes. However," and his voice became stern, "if indeed a student from our school is involved the consequences will be very harsh. As you know, we have a special arrangement with the resort as we are the only high school in the region. Many of you have taken advantage of the discounted seasons passes. Mr. Sorenson made it quite clear that any additional incidents of youth crime will result in our losing these privileges. So if you know of anything, or see anything as you use the facilities, you owe it to the rest of the kids who make use of the resort and don't get involved in such foolishness, to let me know immediately."

I felt a flush of guilt. So our little ruse to make the Ski Patrol hut break in look like a random snowball fight had failed. But what about the other stuff? We certainly had nothing to do with busting windows on the office, or spray painting. I tried to keep my expression neutral. I was hoping my face wasn't red. Then it came.

"Oh, and Tanner?" the principal scanned the class and found me.

"Yes, sir?"

"Come and see me in my office after class, would you?" That was it. I was toast.

On the way down to his office I tried to think of a plausible story. I couldn't. I decided to play it cool and just deny any accusations.

"Come on in." He motioned me inside. He didn't seem too angry. I hadn't been called down to the office for anything before, but I would have expected him to shut the door or start yelling straight away or something. He did none of those things. "I'm trying to meet with your friends Trevor and Xavier today as well," he said.

Uh-oh, I thought.

"It's been a few weeks since your friend Jonas passed away," he said. "I wanted to check in with each of you and see how you were doing."

OK, I thought to myself. That's what this is about. "I'm OK, I guess," I answered.

"I know you had an injury as well. How's the recovery coming along?'

"Fine."

"And your teacher tells me that you managed to keep up with your schoolwork by telecommute. You have missed quite a bit of time. Any concerns?"

"No. Mr. Ryerson says I haven't missed anything."

"Well then." There was a pause. "If you do want to come and speak with me, you know where to find me."

"OK." I stood up to leave.

"One more thing," he said. "You know most of the students who hold seasons tickets to Sighing Pass. Do you know what SOS stands for? Besides the obvious, of course."

I nearly fell over. "No idea," I answered.

"All right. Thanks, Tanner," he said, and I left his office.

I found the others at lunch, but we were in a kind of awkward position. The principal's speech had prompted a lot of gossip in the halls. I didn't want to be seen skulking off with the other guys. How did the principal hear about SOS? That was secret. Only the other Surfers knew about it, and maybe Mike, but definitely no one else. That was one of the rules. No girlfriends, none of the older guys, nobody but us. We sat in the cafeteria and ate lunch and joined in the speculation with the other kids. Some thought it was guys from the graduation year getting up to some pranks. Some thought it was probably kids here on vacation running around at night, bored. It wasn't until we were on our way to *The Edge* after school that we could really talk about it.

Xav had been called in to the office before the principal's little talk so he hadn't been so freaked out. Besides, he hadn't been with Trevor and me that night.

"I thought for sure he knew," Trev said. "And then when I realized that he wasn't even talking about it I was so glad, dude."

"But what about SOS?" asked Xav. "Why would he ask you that?" I stopped for a second, then started running. Xav made the same connection I did, and sprinted up to me. "It better not be," he gasped.

We tore through the resort area parking lot. Behind it was a reservoir of water for the snowmaking equipment to draw from, and behind that, the big equipment sheds where the grooming machines were kept. Xav split to the left of the building; I went right and I saw it first. I stopped and stared. I heard Xav and Trev come up behind me. Spray painted in black paint in letters a meter high it read: SOS.

We split up and headed our separate ways. I gave it some thought when I got home. The last thing we needed to do was panic. If management or anyone else really knew that it had been Trevor and me who had forced our way into the patrol hut, then the police would have been at our doors before now.

It did mean that someone knew the secret name of our organization. And it could be that it was just one more of the attacks against snowboarders, making them look like vandals. Maybe this new development might even be to our advantage. If they knew about the patrol hut, then they probably knew about the contest.

One thing was bothering me, though. What kind of stuff exactly, had been stolen from the resort?

CHAPTER 24

"Tanner?" It was my mom knocking on my door. It was Wednesday evening and I was typing an e-mail to Mel on my computer. "Can I come in?"

"Yeah" I answered. I pressed send and turned around.

"You've probably forgotten," she said, leaning against the door frame, "but it's my birthday tomorrow and Brent has asked us both to dinner. Are you interested?"

With the contest only days away I really wasn't, but two things crossed my mind. First, I wanted her to think everything was normal. I usually didn't spend all my evenings e-mailing snowboarders all over the province. Second, maybe in casual conversation I could learn something more from Brent about what management had made of the patrol hut break-in.

"Uh, sure."

"Good, he'll come by to pick us up tomorrow evening, at seven. Is everything OK, Tanner?"

"Yeah, yeah," I said. I must have been looking a little too thoughtful. "I, uh, nearly forgot your birthday."

She gave a little laugh. "Like father, like son," she said ruefully, and shut the door.

Even though I spent every extra minute I had going over details with Trevor and Xav, I didn't forget to pick up some flowers for my mom on my way home from school the next day. I knew that would put me in her good books for about a year or so. She made a big fuss unwrapping them and putting them in water. I made a few calls and sent a few more e-mails to Bucky and the gang. All the plans were shaping up well, and the weather forecast was excellent for the weekend.

Brent came by in his sports utility and drove us to the restaurant, my favorite steak house. We joked around on the way there. I really liked the guy. He had made the effort to introduce me to his son Mike years before, when Mike was back from one of his surfing safaris and staying with his dad to save money. I didn't have any brothers and my dad wasn't around at that point, so I guess he was trying to find a substitute for me. Anyway, Mike did let me and my friends hang out with him a bit even then, which was way before we started snowboarding. It was listening to his stories that made us decide we would become Surfers and travel all over the world searching for the perfect wave, just like him.

I wondered if Brent and my mom would ever really get together. As guys went, he was one of the least bad possibilities I could think of. Then the thought of having Mike as a real brother made me feel weird. I stopped myself from thinking about it.

"How did the avalanche course go?" Brent asked.

"Fine."

"Have you and your friends been using what you learned?"

"Not really." I wasn't going to give out even the tiniest hint about the contest. "We're staying in-bounds these days. Snowboarders get blamed for everything."

"Like what?" he smiled up from his plate.

"I haven't heard of anything like that recently," my mom

put in.

I was committed now. If I didn't ask now I couldn't bring up the same subject later.

"Some kids were saying at school that there was a break-in at the resort and some stuff was stolen. The principal came around to all the classes and told us that we might lose our discount at the resort." I concentrated on my plate and took a big mouthful of fries.

"First I've heard of it." said Mom.

"During the monthly inventory of our equipment, it was discovered that some supplies and pieces of gear were missing," Brent explained to her. "No one could account for having expended any of it. Some patrollers thought it might be linked to a broken window we had a few weeks back."

I didn't know where to look. I decided to play innocent. "What got stolen?" I asked.

Brent shrugged. "I'm not sure. No painkillers or drugs, though. Nothing was missed right away."

"Any explosives, or anything like that?"

Brent looked at me more seriously. "I'm really not sure. My assistant is handling the incident. Why do you ask? Are the kids at school saying anything about it?"

I realized I wasn't going to get any more useful information from him, and I had probably drawn too much attention to myself. Time to change the subject. "Nope. Just wondered. I haven't heard anything." I stirred the ice in my glass with my straw. "Can I have another Coke, please?" I asked.

The conversation turned to plans Brent and my mom were starting to make for the summer. They were thinking of taking the ferry over to Vancouver Island and hiking the West Coast Trail. Mom asked me if I wanted to go.

"How about Long Beach?" I suggested. "We could camp near there. You could go whale watching, maybe."

My mom raised an eyebrow. "And you could go surfing, maybe?"

Brent laughed. "Watch out, Sally. This is how it starts. The next thing you know you're getting a fax from Fiji asking for some emergency cash." My mom just laughed.

For the rest of dinner we talked about other stuff. I didn't raise the subject of Sighing Pass again.

The rest of the week before the contest flew by. It seemed I was always in a hurried conference with the other Surfers or e-mailing Jenny about something. By the time Friday night came, I felt I couldn't do one more thing. If it wasn't done, then it wasn't ever going to get done. It was hard to get to sleep. I stared at the ceiling and thought about Jonas.

I didn't need my alarm clock the next morning, I had been waking up every hour all night long. I was so restless that Connor had given up sleeping in my room and had gone elsewhere. I wondered about all the boarders in Sighing Pass just for this day. Were they thinking about the same things I was? Probably not, all they were here for was a contest. They weren't thinking about conspiracy, or sabotage, or how to catch a criminal. How did this happen to me? All I was trying to do was ride with my friends, make some sense out of losing Jonas, that's all. And now here I was, a sixteen year old kid, with the whole future of Sighing Pass riding on my shoulders, whether people knew it or not. I looked at the clock. It was 6:00 a.m.. Time to go.

Jenny was staying at the Sighing Pass youth hostel with a bunch of the other riders. I didn't want my mom knowing that today was anything but an ordinary day. It looked like an ordinary day, as I walked down into town. The sun was just starting to come up and the light was gray. There were a few centimeters of fresh powder on top of everything, and the town looked like it was wearing a clean white blanket. I could see lights in a few houses on the way. People were waking up and getting ready for the day. Such an innocent-looking place. And I had thought it just that, an innocent place, up until when, just six weeks ago? It didn't seem so innocent anymore. Jonas was gone forever, dead at sixteen. A violent, terrifying death. People were afraid to ski on the mountain. Hanging out with my friends and riding the mountain would never be something I would take for granted again.

There were lights on at *The Edge of Reason* when I arrived. Mike was tuning up a snowboard and there was a huge stack waiting. All the visiting riders wanted their gear to be in perfect condition for the contest. Trevor, Bucky, and Jenny were sitting on the couches. The usual light-hearted chatter was missing from the group. Everyone looked very serious. Jenny looked up and smiled at me. I winked at her.

"'Morning, Tanner."

"Morning. Is everyone ready for this?" All eyes met mine and there were nods of agreement. "OK.. Let's just do a quick check. Bucky? How's the site?"

"Me and the boys went in yesterday afternoon," he replied. "I don't think any of the lifties suspected anything. We built a sweet little kicker right near the bottom. And there's a snowdrift forming a natural quarter pipe. Dudes should be able to get some good air off that. Looks awesome. I'm totally stoked."

"Did you speak to Mel yet?"

"Just radioed in. He and his team mates stayed up top at

the lodge last night, and headed over at first light. They've dug one pit, everything looks fine. They're going to dig another one lower down. You'll see a green flag if everything's OK."

"Trevor and Jenny?"

They held up their radio beacons.

"Armed and dangerous," said Trevor.

"I've got yours right here," added Jenny, "and Xavier already has his. I found us a frequency to use that no one in the area should be on. It's illegal to use it, though."

"Thanks," I said. "Mike? How about you?"

"My radio's right here, and I'll be here all day, Tanner. If you're right about this and you need help, all you have to do is buzz me and I'll call the police."

"Thanks for doing this," I said appreciatively. I turned to the others. "Now, remember, after we're in position, only use the radios in an emergency and keep any transmission to a minimum. We don't want a burst of static to give any of us away." Everyone nodded. I turned to Jenny. "Where is Xavier, anyway?"

She shook her head slowly. "I don't know," she replied. "He came by the youth hostel last night to pick up the stuff. He said he might not make it here this morning but that we could count on him."

"Dude's probably in position already," offered Trevor. "You know Xav and his alpine starts. It's pretty unlikely that the guy slept in. He's probably dug us all cozy little perches on the ridge already."

"You're probably right," I said. "OK. Let's go. Good luck everybody." Everyone nodded, too nervous to say much. In silence, we gathered our snowboard gear.

CHAPTER 25

From my rocky hiding place I didn't have the greatest view. I couldn't see any of the other Surfers but I could see down into the bowl. It was crowded with riders boarding down, and then climbing slowly up with their snowboards on their backs. They looked like streams of ants carrying pieces of leaf up the sides of the bowl. I wished I were one of them, carefree on a sunny winter morning, doing what I loved best - riding hard down a snowy mountain with my friends.

Bucky and the other judges had the contest under control. It was a low-tech kind of effort and they would be using colored flags to wave riders down the hill. One by one, they would drop into the bowl off a gentle cornice at the top, and begin their run for the judges. I waited for the contest to begin. There was a bit of wind across the ridge and I couldn't hear anything of what was going on, although it seemed still enough in the bowl. I shifted my weight uncomfortably in my perch. I was really wedged in and getting cramped, but I couldn't stand up or move much for fear of being spotted. I'd already radioed my exact location to Mike. There was nothing else to do. I wondered how Jenny and Trevor were doing. What if nothing happened? What if something happened and we missed seeing it? I scanned the snow on all sides. Nothing.

The waiting was killing me. And there was still no sign of Xav.

Movement caught my eye in the bowl and I saw that the contest was starting. The first rider got a green flag and it was time for his run. I saw a tiny figure start the descent. I brought the tiny DVD camcorder to my eye and trained it on the rider. The slope was steep enough at the top there to really lay it out, and the rider leaned hard into his turns, dragging the occasional mitt for show. Flumes of snow flew up behind his racing form. As the slope leveled out a little bit, he could show off his own style more easily. He cruised the slope looking for the best line and popped some air off a couple of bumps. Then he set himself at a five meter rock band and gathered himself for take off. I could see the tension in his body as he corrected his balance and bent his knees. I became aware of my own heart pounding, as if I was the one on the descent. With a sudden shower of snow, he burst over the cliff edge into space and grabbed his toe rail in a classic stance with the other arm boned out over his back.

He hit the landing perfectly and shifted smoothly into a turn. As the slope flattened out some more, he headed for the natural quarter pipe and hit it square; popping into the air for a loose eggflip. He finished off his run by hitting the kicker and I heard a faint applause. It was a pretty cool run by someone who obviously had a lot of backcountry boarding experience.

One by one the other riders dropped in, riding the bowl in their own style. Some turned in tight little arcs, others carved sweeping curves down the mountain. There were a few craggy outcrops, and the landings seemed good on almost all of them. Riders would show themselves to be skilled in carving, or taking big air, or on the quarter pipe. There were some pretty wild wipe-outs too, as riders tumbled through the deep snow. Everyone rode down in his or her own way. I was totally impressed by the women riders who were identified by a purple flag. They were taking some totally audacious lines. I bet Jenny was wishing she was one of them today, had she been able to see them from her hiding place lower down the mountain at the tree line.

Suddenly there was a burst of static from my radio. I heard Jenny's whispered voice.

"Tanner! Look up! There's someone heading up to the ridge! I heard him pass by my spot about five minutes ago but I couldn't see who it was because I had to keep my head down. He should be coming into your sight any minute!"

"Roger." I replied as briefly as possible. I looked at my GPS display. Whoever it was must be following the same route up from the valley that Xav, Trevor and I had taken back from our reconnaissance mission. If he'd passed Jenny's position five minutes before, he should be cresting the ridge in about another ten. I shifted my position so I could aim the camera along the route we had ascended.

It was the longest ten minutes of my life. My thighs were screaming with the strain of crouching in a ready position. I could barely wait to see who would appear on the ridge and yet I felt strangely relieved. There was someone out there. My suspicions had been right all along.

It was Jeff all right. I could tell the moment his ski tips appeared over the ridge. Those unmistakable fat yellow powder skis I'd first seen on a work bench in Mike's shop. He was dressed in a loose white jacket and pants, and a white hat. I guessed he was trying to camouflage himself against the snow while he laid his charges of explosives. I felt oddly calm. I pressed the speak button on the radio so an unexpected transmission couldn't give away my position, and I waited. I kept the camera rolling.

Just then a second hat appeared over the crest of the hill, followed by a figure in a yellow Ski Patrol jacket. I held my breath and squinted to see who it was, but the man was looking down and I couldn't see his face. I could hear him breathing heavily as he drew nearer. Then he stopped and looked up to speak to Jeff. I nearly dropped the camera.

"Bloody hell, this is hard work," he said, in an unmistakable Irish accent.

I froze. *What are we supposed to do now?* My heart was pounding so loudly I was afraid they would overhear. *There are only two of us! Where's Xav?*

"We'll hike around behind the ridge and set the charges up on the east lip." Jeff was pointing at what I knew was a huge overhanging cornice. "There's enough snow up there cause these idiots some serious technical difficulties."

"One well placed charge ought to do the trick," Brent was saying, when I heard an agonized shout.

"Brent! How could you?" It was Trevor, standing up from his cramped hiding place only meters from the two patrollers. "You murderer! You murdered Jonas!"

"What the bloody hell?" I heard Brent say, as Trevor started to charge towards them.

Trevor's sudden outburst compelled me to act. Keeping low and trying to keep out of sight I held the radio transceiver to my mouth and whispered as fiercely as possible into the microphone. "S.O.S! S.O.S! They're here! Two of them! Mike, call the police!"

I stood up just in time to see Jeff take a swing at Trevor. I heard the blow as it connected and Trevor dropped to his knees. As he started to rise, blood streaming from his nose, Jeff aimed a kick at him. I dropped everything, grabbed my board and ran towards them, shouting.

"It's over, Brent! I've radioed the police!" I came to a stop in front of them. "Forget it, man. It's over." I was shaking.

Brent gave a wry laugh. "You too, you stupid lad? Over?" He sneered. "Do you have any idea what you've gotten yourself into?" I heard Jeff kick Trevor again. He groaned and tried to stand up. "Leave them, Jeff. Let's get out of here. No one's going to believe these punks anyway. What can a couple of snowboarders do, shred us?"

"Leave them? Are you crazy? I came prepared for this." I felt suddenly numb. In Jeff's hand was a pistol and he was pointing it at Trevor, lying on the snow. "We'll throw the bodies down a couloir. Everyone will think they took one risk too many." He aimed another kick at Trevor's huddled form, but this time Trevor was ready.

"Murderer!" he screamed as he grabbed Jeff's ski boot, and with a heave pulled him off balance, knocking him on his back. I saw the pistol fly out of Jeff's hand and disappear into the powder. Brent was on Trevor in an instant, pushing his face down into the snow.

I swung my board around in a wide arc with all my strength. With a crack it connected with Brent's forehead, opening up a long gash and laying him out flat on his back. He didn't move. Trevor had struggled to his knees. He was pointing past me and speaking, but my heart was pounding so incredibly loud I couldn't hear his words. Then I turned and suddenly understood what it was that was pounding.

First the rotors appeared over the crest of the ridge, then

the bright red paint of the Alpine Air helicopter. I closed my eyes and opened them again. It was still there. The chopper tilted as it approached us and I could see faces turned towards us and fingers pointing. I stared up at it.

There was Mr. Dupuis at the controls with the missing Xavier beside him. Between them there was an angry face I knew from somewhere. It took me a moment to place him. It was Karl Sorenson. the Area Manager. Beside him was someone else I didn't recognize.

I sat back in the snow and felt relief wash through me. The chopper moved in to hover above us and I squinted my eyes against the hail of snow and icy pellets the rotors kicked up. I saw Brent sit up from where he was lying in the snow, shake his fist at the machine overhead and scream at it, but the noise and wind from the rotors whipped away the sound.

I felt a sudden yank on my sleeve and turned to Trevor. Somehow he had the gun in his hand and had it aimed at Brent. With the other he was frantically pointing down the mountainside. I looked. Jeff had his skis on and he was getting away!

CHAPTER 26

What came next was pure reaction. Desperately, I stomped into my snowboard bindings and jumped to turn the tip of the board downhill. I could barely see a thing with the snow whipping around. There was no way I was going to let Jeff get away. As I moved out from the disturbance caused by the helicopter, I saw that he was about fifteen meters ahead of me. He headed straight down towards the tree line and I followed. We both picked up tons of speed, but my wide board rode atop the powder and I gained a few meters on him.

Then we were in the trees and he disappeared. I could see where he'd gone as the trees ahead of me moved and showers of snow knocked from the branches exploded in clouds. The snow was deep and the trees were thick.

Oh man, was he ever good! It was so steep and I was riding at the extreme limit of my ability. I would crank a turn around a tree and only barely have time to avoid the next. Branches tore at my face and caught my clothing. At times I was carried on a shifting, sliding slab of snow. I passed one of his ski poles, planted deeply in the slope and wrenched out of his grip, then the other one. I realized he must be barely hanging on himself.

Then he burst out of the trees ahead and I followed. I

caught a glimpse of rock, space and then a gully below. I had an instant to gather myself and then I was airborne over a five-meter cliff. I saw him land below me, arms flailing as he tried to keep his balance. He flung forwards and started to cart-wheel. I landed hard and threw the board into a turn to try to slow down. I dug my heel edge as hard as I could into the powder. Jeff tumbled down towards some jagged rocks at the end of the gully, and towards the open space beyond. Desperately, I leaned back even further, snow spraying up into my face. I saw Jeff's body, limp as a rag doll's, strike the rocks and flip over out of sight. My board chattered at the edge of control as I slid towards the same fate. I dug my edge in with all my strength. Finally, I felt my board slow beneath me, and I came to a stop lying on my back.

Then I heard it, the unmistakable "CRACK!" below me as the snow slope gave way, followed by the deafening rumble of millions of tons of snow roaring down the mountainside. An enormous cloud of snow rose up around me and blocked out the sun.

In this world of white, I traversed carefully to the relative safety of a rock outcrop on the side of the gully, and there I sat for a moment. I took off my board and stood it upright in the snow. I leaned back against the rock and closed my eyes until I felt my pounding heart slow down. My knee throbbed. I waited until the snow settled and I could feel the warm sun on my face again. Then, as if in a dream, I reached inside my jacket and pulled out the radio.

EPILOGUE

"Nice one, Jenny!" I yelled. She did another 180° off the lip of the halfpipe and finished her run. "Not bad!" I said.

"She's getting pretty good," said Trevor, beside me. I looked around at the all the jumps, barrels, poles and other stuff. Snowboarders never had it so good. Sighing Pass' new pipe dragon did an awesome job maintaining the pipe at the Jonas Wilson Memorial Snowboard Park. There were riders coming up from the city all the time to hone their jumps and tricks, and lots of kids in town were getting into it. Jenny was smiling at me. Her face was tanned from spending the March break holiday on a snowboard under the spring sun. I couldn't see her eyes behind her narrow sunglasses.

"They've just groomed the hill. Let's go carve some corduroy and get something to eat at the lodge. You wanna come, Trevor?"

"Naw, thanks," he replied. "Riding corduroy makes my board fart. I'll see you guys later." He turned off towards one of the jumps.

Jenny and I undid our back bindings and pedaled up to the high speed quad chairlift. We sat in the two center seats. I brought down the safety bar so we could rest our boards on it and I put my arm around her. I looked across the hill.

Things sure had changed a lot in the last six weeks since Brent's arrest and Jeff's disappearance. Caught red-handed with a pack full of explosives, Brent had made a full confession.

It turned out that he and Jeff had been hired by Nathan Pride of the Ski Northwest Corporation to sabotage Sighing Pass' reputation by engineering "freak" accidents and making them seem as if they'd been caused by chance, neglect, or natural causes. Bitter about being underpaid and unacknowledged as a Ski Patroller, he had stood to make a great deal of money when Ski Northwest finally acquired Sighing Pass for a fraction of its true market value. His arrest caused a real stir in town. My mom still couldn't believe how badly she'd been duped. She'd thought he was a total gentleman the entire time that he'd been using her as a way of getting information about us snowboarders. Not to mention that he'd tried to arrange for my "accidental" death. I felt kind of sorry for her.

Most of all though, I felt sorry for Mike, who had no idea when he'd relayed my message to the police that one the criminals he was helping to catch was his own father.

Xavier had once again established his genius. The fourth man in the helicopter that day had been the insurance inspector. He'd not only convinced his father to arrange to take him on an aerial tour of the resort and its back bowls with the inspector and the resort manager that day, but also to follow his G.P.S. co-ordinates over to the ridge where our ambush took place.

Experts had been called in and it was proven that the snowpack at Sighing Pass was no more likely to avalanche due to the formation of depth hoar than any other resort in the Coastal Range. The publicity had been a positive thing for the resort and business returned. Mr. Sorenson was so grateful to the Surfers that he'd given us all season's passes to the place. He was taking Nathan Pride and Ski Northwest to court, and expected to win such a large settlement that he'd gone ahead and started building the wickedest snowboard park in the region.

Not that all the news was great. Jonas was still gone and he was never coming back. His death had been the key to unraveling the whole mystery but he would never know of it. He'd never carve turns down a mountain again and he'd never get to drop into the pipe in the snowboard park named after him. That left a bitter taste in my mouth. And now Jenny was about to drop another piece of bad news.

"Tanner, you know that paper I wrote for the science competition? The one about depth hoar?" She turned to face me on the chair lift.

"Yeah."

"Well, it won the competition."

"That's awesome!" I gave her a kiss. "Congratulations! What do you win?"

"Ummm. That's kind of the bad news."

"What do you mean?"

"The prize is to go on a student exchange. For a year."

I felt my heart sink. "Oh, yeah? Where to?"

"Well, France actually. Chamonix, to be exact. In the Alps."

"Wow," I said thoughtfully, looking out at the familiar peaks of the Coastal Range. I'd never boarded anyplace else. Maybe it was time to broaden my horizons a little bit, improve my French. And, well, Chamonix was the ultimate road trip destination for snowboarders. I smiled and snuggled her a little closer to me. "Chamonix, eh?"

End

CHECK THESE OUT...

Canadian Avalanche Association
P.O. Box 2759
Revelstoke,British Columbia
Canada
V0E 2SO
Tel. 250-837-2435
www.avalanche.ca

United States Snowboarding Association
P.O. Box 100
Park City, UT
84060
USA
Tel. 801-649-9090

The Canadian Outward Bound Wilderness School
150 Laird Drive
Suite 302
Toronto, Ontario
Canada
M4G 3V7
Tel. 416-421-8111

Canadian Federation of Snowboarding
250 West Beaver Creek Rd.
Unit #1 2nd Floor
Richmond Hill, Ontario
Canada
L4B 1C7
Tel. 905-764-5355